About the Author

Jonathan Reach is the pseudonym for a retired professional living in Wiltshire. He has a large grown-up family living around the world. His interests include walking, golf and cricket which he played at village level to seventy-two. He is a film buff and worked briefly as a film critic in his younger days. In the 60s and 70s, he made a number of amateur films set in Wiltshire.

The Paradise Collection

Jonathan Reach

The Paradise Collection

Vanguard Press

A CIP catalogue record for this title is
available from the British Library.

ISBN 978-1-83794-090-5

Vanguard Press is an imprint of
Pegasus Elliot Mackenzie Publishers Ltd.
www.pegasuspublishers.com

First Published in 2024

Vanguard Press
Sheraton House Castle Park
Cambridge England

Printed & Bound in Great Britain

Chapter One

It was pretty well what he imagined.

A smart and comfortable hotel, with lavish views of the sea and a very civilised ambience.

Robert Granger—Robbie to his friends, acquaintances and past associates—surveyed the view from his comfortable suite on the first floor.

He had been in residence for about two months now, and the management had no idea at all of his past existence.

All they knew is that he had approached them with a very realistic proposal to occupy the suite on a permanent basis.

Faced as they were with many meagre winter months of empty rooms, they were only too glad to negotiate a very fair rate. This would include breakfast and a choice of either lunch or dinner.

The manager, Jean-Claude—you cut his accent with a knife—had run a pension somewhere in France. He was affable and given to expressions of exasperation at any minor setback.

There were eight staff coming and going who took little interest in him.

Apart from himself, there were four residents: Percy Chambers, a retired judge who kept well to himself, Miss Edith Noble, a lady of ninety-odd years who had based herself to a remarkable degree on Miss Marple, Ted Brown, a widowed turf accountant whose smoking habit had started to affect him, and, last but not least, Mrs Rose Staples.

Without a shadow of a doubt, she was of the aristocracy. She had no doubt about it and her sharp, superior manner brooked no argument.

Robert found that at breakfast—when he happened to coincide with Ted—they would exchange a few choice words about the state of the country.

At this reserve, now fifty-eight, Robert felt that he could be as critical as he liked, since neither he, Tom or anyone else of the same disposition, could do a damned thing about it.

The others would nod and look away, unused to the habit of conversation in the early morning.

Not that any of them now bothered to rise at the crack of dawn, something Robert had disciplined himself to do over many years.

Life on the southern side of the Isle of Wight suited him just fine. Far enough away from England to feel rather like abroad, but not in reality.

He had never been married, but several times had come close and had enjoyed—if that is the right word—some spiky relationships.

Problems always arose due to his completely unconventional working hours, and an intransigent streak which eventually spelt disaster.

The past was the past and he had no regrets.

Perhaps he had settled for retirement too early, but he still kept himself in shape with a daily run along the cliffs and a bathe in the sea when he could steel himself to the cold. He was much fitter than the other residents and rather prided himself on it.

Of course, a number of other guests, including family groups, would stay for a little while, disturbing the rhythm of life for the residents.

Jean-Claude had thoughtfully provided a large room at the back of the hotel which was reserved for the residents, and woe betide any guest intruding in this oasis of peace.

Robert could look forward to the future with equanimity.

From time to time, he cast his mind back to his past life and to the extraordinary good fortune that had resulted in his status quo.

Chapter Two

Two years ago

Robert looked around the dump he rather rashly called an office.

The sign on his door indicating 'Private Investigator' leered back at him.

He had been in this game for eight years after a career of sorts in the army.

That had left him with a gratuity and pension which helped in the fairly long intervals between investigations.

He had started off in business with a younger partner but soon came to realise his mistake.

His methods and lack of patience soon led to conflicts and the younger man was shortly out of the door.

There was only one way to conduct his business and it was his own way.

As an investigator, he advertised, of course, but he never knew how his reputation went before him.

His contacts in the army were helpful, but the police locally viewed him with rather a bleary eye.

He had come into conflict with them after a punch-up relating to his apprehending an errant husband, but, as he pointed out after they picked up the miscreant from the floor, he was only doing his job.

It was, however, pleasing to be reminded that when push came to shove, he could look after himself.

On a September Tuesday, he was inspecting his latest bank statement with some concern, when he saw the outline of a woman standing outside his door.

She hesitated for half a minute before firmly knocking on the door.

He got up swiftly to let her in, finding that she was a well-dressed, attractive woman in her early fifties.

She swept into the room as though she owned it and confronted Robert.

'Mr Granger?' she enquired imperiously.

He nodded in reply rather taken aback, and recovered enough to offer her a chair facing his desk.

She settled there, looking rather doubtfully at the surroundings.

'I understand that you are a private investigator.'

'That's what it says on the door.'

This remark, which might have gone down well with a normal client, did not impress.

'You have been recommended to me as someone discreet and determined,' she said.

'Thank you.'

He was about to enquire as to the origin of this boost but held back.

'My name is Flora Jenkins—Mrs Jenkins to you. I have a job for you. I'm afraid it will not be very pleasant and it may not be easy.'

Curiousity aroused, Robert waited for her to continue.

She paused while taking out a cigarette holder, which appeared expensive, and slotting in a cigarette.

Robert leaned forward to give her a light.

She inhaled deeply, exhaled the smoke very deliberately and carried on.

'My husband, Gerald, is a naughty boy. He has been playing away through much of our married life, but we have always reconciled.

'The last time—with his secretary—he promised faithfully that this would be the last.

'I took him at his word—though God knows why based on past experience, but I still loved him.

'Mr Granger, I am not in good health. I have suffered through these infidelities and it has dragged me down.

'Now I understand on good authority that he is cheating again. This is the last straw.

'He is extremely devious and knows by now how to cover his tracks.

'My mission for you is to find out the identity of his current squeeze— who she is, where they are meeting and I need some positive proof to confront him.

'Expense is no object—I am a wealthy woman.

'Will you help me?'

Robert had been listening closely and now knew that there was possibly a large payday ahead of him.

'Mrs Jenkins, I will do everything I can to help; you can rely on me.'

She sank visibly into the chair and seemed to shrink.

She turned a tearful eye to Robert.

'I am so grateful. Now, let me tell you about my husband to give you a headstart.'

Chapter Three

'On second thoughts, I would prefer to brief you on my own turf.'

Flora Jenkins delved into her capacious handbag and brought out a card which she handed to Robert with a flourish.

'That's my address—Gerald is away overnight so I suggest that you call on me about five.'

'Of course.'

Robert stood at attention while Flora rose majestically, turned and offered a highly perfumed hand.

A moment later, she swept out and was gone, leaving an expensive-scented aroma in her wake.

Robert glanced at the card which read,

Gerald and Flora Jenkins

Southey Manor

Hyde

No telephone number was volunteered.

Robert knew that Hyde was a very exclusive area up in the hills where most of the properties were enormous with extensive grounds.

He had rarely ventured there. The inhabitants tended to deal in millions and were well above his pay grade.

It was an enormous compliment to him that Flora Jenkins would entrust him with their problems.

He spent the morning sorting out his finances, ate a light lunch at his favourite local pub, and decided to case the Hyde area.

It was a thirty-minute drive, at first, through the suburbs and, then as he climbed into the hills, the traffic thinned to the occasional Bentley.

At a quarter to five, he approached the double gates of Southey Manor, got out and went to the intercom to announce his arrival.

There was a crackling on the other end, before a male voice in a heavy foreign accent invited him to identify himself.

There was then a long interval before the gates slowly opened, revealing an immaculate driveway.

He was only too aware of the incongruous nature of his old Ford Tourneo as he made his way slowly up to the manor house—a vast property of late Victorian design.

He parked outside the steps leading up to a surprisingly modern front door and rang the bell.

Almost immediately it opened to reveal the male servant who had spoken at the gate.

He was invited in and led along a passageway into the vast living room where Flora Jenkins stood against an imposing fireplace.

She waved the servant away with a slight gesture and came forward to welcome Robert.

'It's time for my gin and tonic—can I offer you one? The accent for me at least is heavily on the gin,' she said.

'I would like that very much,' Robert answered.

It was not his tipple—beer or whisky were his habit—but how could he refuse such an offer?

Flora walked across to the wall cabinet, which he noticed was filled to capacity with every kind of alcoholic drink.

She poured them both a long G and T and certainly did not stint on the G.

She waved him to a sumptuous settee and settled there.

'Now, to business. Gerald is the buyer for a large concern with connections worldwide so he travels a lot.

'He does not always make me privy to his programme but, this time, I know that tomorrow he is off to Northern Ireland for a meeting in Belfast, then travelling by train to Dublin the following day.

'I am extremely suspicious that he has an assignation at his hotel tomorrow or in Dublin.

'I want you to follow and find out for me—no expense spared.

'Do whatever you have to do—but I intend to nail him this time.'

Chapter Four

On the way back, Robert passed the time by enumerating his favourite 'hates' of life as he lived from day to day.

Number one was the number of 'L' drivers haunting the roads around town. Obviously one had to learn to drive, but did there need to be so many around at once holding up traffic?

Second, was people with two or more dogs on long leads who did not control them and caused you to take evading action.

Again, Robert resented people with those dogs, hauling them around his favourite pubs and restaurants, which he considered unsanitary and made a mockery of the establishments having top marks for hygiene.

Number four was people as one walked along, who approached while staring intently at their phone and never looking up to see where they are going.

Next were drivers who insisted on backing into meagre parking spaces which they were incompetent to do properly, taking two or three stabs at it and holding up all the following traffic.

He felt that was enough to be going on with—the frustrations of modern life—not to mention the endless roadworks and diversions everywhere.

Flora Jenkins had given him enough information to enable him to book a flight to Belfast the following morning.

He was armed with a rather flattering photo of Gerald—and noticed immediately the disparity in ages between him and Flora.

Perhaps this was the root cause of his endless philandering.

Robert was highly experienced in discreet pursuits and carried with him a pack of items which he may need for surveillance over a long period.

The following morning, he drove to the airport and went through the endless security procedures, keeping a wary eye out for Gerald.

In the departure lounge, he soon spotted him standing and talking to a male colleague.

As they entered the plane, he found himself about four rows back from his target.

Flora had tipped him that when in Belfast—which Gerald frequented—he would usually stay at the Hilton.

Robert was able to book himself into a single room at some expense.

As he collected his luggage, travelling very light, he noticed Gerald making for the taxi rank and followed close enough to grab the next cab in line.

Gerald decamped from his cab just as Gerald was pulling up.

He dawdled for a few minutes, allowing time for Gerald to book into reception.

On arrival, the desk was clear for a moment and Robert took a quick look at the register, noting that Gerald would be occupying room twenty-six on the first floor.

He ascended the stairs to his own room – by chance on the same floor.

This gave time for Gerald to go up in the lift without encountering him.

As Robert reached his room he saw Gerald up the corridor opening his door.

It was nine thirty and Robert assumed that Gerald's business meeting would be starting soon in the hotel's conference room which he had used himself in the past.

Flora had armed him with the name of Gerald's company and a telephone enquiry of reception told him that the meeting was timed for ten o'clock.

He noted that a second company dealing in women's expensive accessories had a meeting timed for ten-thirty in another part of the hotel.

Robert went down to reception and parked himself adjacent to the meeting room at about ten o'clock, as instinct told him that Gerald's intended assignation might well involve someone from this company.

Sure enough, after a few minutes, a group of young women assembled.

Their strikingly attractive leader led them into the conference room.

Something old Robert that he was now onto something.

He would keep a good eye on her as the day progressed.

Chapter Five

The morning passed pleasantly enough, with Robert walking quietly to and fro keeping an eye on the progress of the meetings.

After a while, he decided to concentrate on the second meeting.

He had no idea when it would end but the time had moved on to twelve-thirty.

As he sat near the entrance, the door burst open and the attractive leader emerged, followed by her team.

As they passed him, a messenger from the hotel hurried up and announced that he had a message for Miss Dolman.

'That's for you, Liz,' said one of the team.

The message, on a slip of paper, was duly delivered and now Robert knew her identity—Elizabeth Dolman.

The job had been done for him at a stroke.

Next on the agenda was lunch.

Robert would not normally have eaten midday but he needed to keep a close eye on Gerald and Elizabeth.

Once in the spacious dining room, the two teams sat at large tables a little away from each other.

Robert sat alone at a small table, keeping his eyes open.

He had already used his phone to take a clear picture of Elizabeth for the record.

There were some appetising choices on the menu and Robert ended up having steak and chips followed by a delicious Eton mess.

He noticed that from time to time, Gerald's gaze settled briefly on Elizabeth, and it was clear that she was aware of this but trying not to draw attention to herself.

Lunch over, the parties began to rise from their tables and Robert watched as Gerald left the room and made for the lift.

After about five minutes, Elizabeth excused herself from her team and also approached the lift.

This was crunch time, and Robert now moved swiftly to the stairs, hoping to reach the first floor before Gerald.

As he emerged onto the first floor, he was just in time to see Gerald disappearing into his room.

He kept out of sight waiting for Elizabeth, who, sure enough, stepped out of the lift, walked calmly down the corridor and, after glancing round as Robert photographed her again on his phone, tapped gently on Gerald's door.

After a moment, the door opened and she slipped inside.

Robert walked up and took another shot of the door and its number.

Now he had to decide whether to wait—perhaps for hours—until Elizabeth emerged from her tryst.

He had nowhere to hide and felt that he had accomplished his mission.

It was simply a question of confirming the identity and address of the company for whom Elizabeth was working, which the assistant manager divulged to him having been slipped a quick tenner.

He was due to fly on to Dublin should Gerald have failed to meet anyone here, but there was obviously no need.

He managed to arrange a flight back to England late that night.

The next morning, he phoned Flora Jenkins.

She was surprised to hear from him so soon.

'I have information for you,' he said.

It was clear from this that Flora expected the worst, but she had sent him on his mission and must face up to the bitter truth.

Chapter Six

This was the part that Robert always dreaded.

On the one hand, he had the satisfaction of a job well done, but it was dirty work, and someone was going to be badly hurt.

Perhaps it was her natural reluctance to hear distressing news on the phone, but Flora insisted that Robert come and see her straight away.

He travelled the distance feeling low and rather depressed.

The gates of Southey Manor opened and he crept up the drive at a slow pace.

As he approached the manor, he saw that Flora was already outside the front door waiting for him.

She seemed remarkably composed as she greeted him cordially and led him into the house.

'Tell me the worst,' she said suddenly.

'I want to know everything—don't hold back. I can take it—it's not the first time.'

There was nothing for it.

Robert related the whole story, showing Flora the pictures he had taken. She gasped as she saw Elizabeth.

'She's so young. They're getting younger all the time.'

Her disappearing into Gerald's room left no doubt as to their intentions.

Flora began to cry—huge sobs that nearly broke Robert's heart, inured as he was to this scenario as part of his profession.

'In my heart, I knew that I could still not trust him—in spite of my warning him that this would be the last time.

'I'll confront him with this when he returns on Sunday. I'm very grateful to you, Mr Granger.

'You did splendidly. I shall always be grateful for your efforts. Now I have to decide what to do.'

'I'm dreadfully sorry to bring you this bad news,' said Robert.

'No, no, it's a relief. I've been kidding myself for far too long.'

'I had better be going unless I can do anything more for you,' said Robert rather pointlessly.

He turned to leave when Flora came across and suddenly planted a kiss on his cheek.

'Please send me your account—I'll settle it straight away. I shall recommend your services with absolute confidence should the opportunity arise.'

There was nothing more to be said which could help her.

Ahead was the awful period of waiting to confront the man she still loved who was incapable of being faithful to her.

Robert retraced his steps back to town with a heavy heart.

The whole enterprise had not been very costly, by his usual standards.

He sent Flora his bill in the post and was gratified to receive a cheque by return—with a considerable bonus which would see him through thin times ahead.

He heard nothing more for the next six months.

Then, one day, he received a call.

'Mr Granger, I'm Mrs Flora Jenkins's lawyer. I have some bad news for you. Mrs Jenkins passed away on Tuesday of last week. However, it is not all bad news for you.

'I have her will in front of me. She has left you a considerable legacy. You are in no way related?'

'No, not at all. I did some work for her a few months ago but have not heard from her since.'

The lawyer seemed rather surprised.

'Well, I have no doubt you are aware that Mrs Jenkins was a very wealthy woman.'

'I understand so,' said Robert, awaiting the punch line that he knew was coming.

'There are a number of legacies. So far as I can calculate at present, on the basis that there are various securities to realise, the estimate is about one million four hundred.'

'It will take a while to sort out the estate but I will contact you further in due course.'

Robert got up and whooped around the office.

'God bless you, Flora Jenkins,' he repeated over and over again.

Now his life would change forever.

Chapter Seven

To live in anticipation of a life-changing event is like an endless dream.

Life goes on from day to day as normal, but with the expectation that this is only temporary.

Robert heard nothing more from the lawyer and began to wonder whether he had imagined their conversation.

He had no contact with anyone in Flora Jenkins's family, her friends or her relations.

He had no idea whether, on his return from Ireland, she had confronted him and thrown him out of the house, which he thoroughly deserved.

Work had dried up over the autumn, and he had started to wonder what exactly he would do with the inheritance—if it ever arrived.

He was aware that probate could be a lengthy process, and depended on the efficiency of the law firm involved.

He had almost given up when a letter arrived the following spring.

There—at last—was a cheque for the princely sum of one million, four hundred and ten thousand pounds.

Imagine going into the bank and paying such a sum—he would certainly do this with a flourish just to see their faces.

Now he could plan in earnest.

He had always wanted to retire one day to the Isle of Wight, where he had enjoyed several holidays as a child.

He had no family—both his parents were gone and his only relatives were two sisters living with their families in Australia and thriving.

He would see them about once a year but had no ambitions to go down under.

He searched the internet for suitable hotels on the south coast of the Isle of Wight and found one that appeared ideal—not too large and impressive looking with the beach nearby.

Rather than judge from afar, he closed down the office and took a break, arranging to stay for a few days.

He was greeted by Jean-Claude, the manager, and very soon found his way around the hotel and the immediate area, including the good beach nearby.

There seemed to be a few residents as well as the holiday guests, who paid him little attention.

The food was good and he had the chance to view a comfortable suite on the first floor which would suit him down to the ground.

At the end of his stay, he assessed the likely cost of booking himself permanently into the suite.

There were few guests at the time and he figured that there would be periods when most of the hotel's fourteen rooms would be empty.

Having the certainty of his booking would be welcome.

He found Jean-Paul was a businessman but also practical and after a bit of good-natured haggling, they agreed to a price on a weekly basis.

Returning to his office, he decided to give notice immediately to his landlord—one month would suffice—and to advertise the closure of his business.

There was really no goodwill element to pass on, as everything had depended on his skill and reputation.

He sold off what little furniture was of any value and closed down without a backward glance.

He arrived at the hotel with two large cases—effectively these were his life possessions, mostly clothes which had seen better days.

He had already contacted a reliable investment consultant to deal with investing the vast majority of his inheritance with an emphasis on income rather than growth.

He settled in quickly to a daily routine, not for a moment missing his detective work.

Chapter Eight

Life continued in much the same fashion over the next month.

Ted was generally in a cheerful mood and ready for a chat at breakfast.

The others continued to give a slight nod of recognition in the mornings.

Robert continued with his routine of a run along the cliffs, and a bathe in the sea in the late morning before lunch.

He noticed that the Judge would quite often take a stroll along the beach coinciding with Robert's bathe.

This appeared to be the only exercise the old boy took, spending the rest of the day in the residents' lounge reading the papers or poring over a book.

Occasionally, Edith Noble would exchange an odd word with him, but Rose Staples often took breakfast in her room and was rarely seen.

On a sunny Friday morning, Robert set off as usual for his late morning swim.

The water seemed warmer than usual and he crawled out further into the sea than usual.

It must have been ten or fifteen minutes later that he emerged and started off up the beach. About thirty metres from the sea, he saw what appeared to be a body face down on the sand.

He hurried forward and found that it was the Judge, sporting a large gash on the back of his head that was bleeding profusely.

There was no sign of anyone about.

The Judge appeared to be unconscious, and Robert knelt down to check that he was still breathing.

The old boy was thankfully still alive.

Robert left him and ran up to the hotel to alert Jean-Claude and ring for an ambulance.

They had no idea how long this would take, so they both set off for the beach and placed a blanket over the Judge's body.

The site of the injury left them in no doubt that the Judge had been taken unawares by his assailant and struck a heavy blow from behind.

Robert's history in the army had made him very familiar with injuries of every kind.

Although the Judge was still breathing, it could well be that the blow was intended to kill.

Robert remained with the body while Jean-Claude returned to the hotel to ring the police.

He hesitated to touch the wound.

Unsurprisingly, it was the police who arrived first on the scene.

'I am Detective Sergeant Ruddock and this is DC Cook.'

Robert looked up to see them standing over him.

'Who found the body?' Sergeant Ruddock enquired.

Robert explained that he had noticed the Judge lying on the sand as he emerged from his swim.

'Did you notice anyone else around—before or after your swim?'

'No, the beach was deserted. Presumably, the Judge was taking his usual walk when it happened.'

'So, this was a habit of his—every morning?'

'Usually, yes. As long as the weather was fine.'

'So, others would have known where to find him.'

She inquired about the other residents and their habits.

'I've never seen any of them venture to the beach' said Robert. 'They are not ones for exercise.'

The Sergeant nodded.

'What about guests staying at the hotel?'

'It's quiet at the moment. I think there is only one family—husband, wife and two young children under school age.'

At that moment, two ambulance men arrived on the scene and immediately took charge of the body.

'He's unconscious but appears to be breathing okay. Can we take him now or are you needing to do some scenes of crime work?'

'Give us a few minutes,' the Sergeant replied.

Jean-Claude had joined the throng and identified himself.

'I would like you to close the hotel for new visitors and ask all the residents to remain where they are until we have had the opportunity to interview them.'

Jean-Claude nodded and went off to break the bad news.

Chapter Nine

The rest of the morning was taken up by scenes of crime and a group of other officers down at the beach, with some of them looking nearby to see if they could locate the weapon.

Eventually, an uneven piece of rock was discovered thrown into the scrub, on which blood could plainly be seen.

This was taken away to be fingerprinted and tested for DNA.

Robert was able to observe all this activity from the privacy of his suite overlooking the beach.

He was also able to appreciate the charms of Detective Sergeant Ruddock, in her smart hat with blonde hair tucked carefully in behind.

She was very much in charge of DC Cook, who simply stood around rather vacantly waiting for orders.

Jean-Claude had apprised the others of the Judge's fate, which greatly upset Edith Noble, who retired in tears to the bathroom.

Ted showed concern, but more for himself as a possible suspect than for the victim.

Rose Staples came to the door of the room, opened it slightly, took in the news and promptly shut the door again in Jean-Claude's face.

Her reaction, whatever it may have been, went unseen.

The family staying for a week in the hotel were visibly shocked and upset that their plans for the day would be upended by the police requiring them to stay put.

After a while, the children could be heard enquiring in a querulous manner why they could not go to the beach to play.

Lunch was a lonely feast with only Robert and Ted in attendance.

'I suppose a judge makes enemies along the way,' said Ted.

'Inevitably, but you don't usually find people taking revenge so long after the event. He must have been retired for over five years,' Robert replied.

'You saw nobody on the beach while you were swimming?'

'I suppose I was facing in the opposite direction most of the time.'

'Do you think they intended to kill him?'

'I think so. At the moment we don't know whether or not he will pull through. If not, it's murder.'

'At the very least, attempted murder. Does that carry a lesser penalty nowadays?'

Robert searched his memory.

'I think it's the same as manslaughter. I think it's life.'

That shut them up and they continued to chew in silence.

As they rose to return to their rooms, they spotted Detective Sergeant Ruddock approaching, followed doggedly by DC Cook.

'She's coming to interview us, I expect,' said Robert.

'At the moment, we are just possible witnesses— not suspects. Otherwise, it would be down at the station under caution—the whole works.'

'I am going to make myself scarce for the moment. They can find me in my room when they want me. I saw nothing and I know nothing.' Ted departed in something of a hurry.

Robert felt this was a bit of a dog-in-a-manger attitude when he imagined they were all keen to help.

He sat down to collect his thoughts.

As the person first on the scene of the crime, he knew that he would be a possible suspect.

The police would be keen to locate a motive for what, on the face of it, appeared to be a pointless crime.

At the time, the Judge was dressed in a shirt and shorts, carrying nothing of value except perhaps for his watch,

Robert had noted that this was expensive—the Judge was never shy of flashing it around—but it had remained firmly on his wrist where he fell.

This was the first thing Robert had noticed as he knelt examining the body.

Detective Sergeant Ruddock entered the dining room.

'I'll want to talk to everybody—but perhaps it would be appropriate to start with you.'

Chapter Ten

The three of them seated themselves comfortably around the centre table in the residents' lounge.

Detective Sergeant Ruddock removed her hat and let her fair hair tumble around her face.

She really was very attractive, thought Robert.

He had to steel himself not to let his guard slip and say something that he would later regret.

DC Cook was ready to take notes.

'Jennifer Ruddock—I'm presently in charge of this investigation but, depending on what progress is made, I may be replaced by someone at a higher level.'

Robert nodded that he understood.

'This is not a formal interview. You are not under caution. DC Cook here will take notes. At this stage, you are a witness—not a suspect.

'Can you begin by telling us again how you came across the victim—retired Judge Percy Chambers.'

'I had been for my morning swim—I was out a bit longer than usual.

'As I reached the beach, I saw a body lying ahead of me. It turned out to be the Judge who I took to have been on his usual morning walk.

'I saw that he had a serious head wound. I checked to find that he was unconscious but alive.

'I went up to the hotel and alerted Jean-Claude, the manager, who called for an ambulance. We then went back together and placed a blanket over the body.

'Jean-Claude then called you and you arrived before the ambulance.'

DC Cook was busy writing all this down.

'Tell me about yourself. How long have you been resident here?'

Robert decided to be absolutely frank with them.

'About two months. I have a permanent residency in a suite on the first floor. I am a retired private detective. I spent some years in the army and then set up on my own.

'About a year ago, I did some work for a wealthy client.

'She was apparently very satisfied with my work, because, shortly afterwards, she died and left me a considerable legacy—enough for me to be able to retire here well before I had expected.'

The sergeant raised her eyebrows.

'Do you expect to stay here for the foreseeable future then?'

'Yes, I have always enjoyed holidays on the island and had planned one day to retire here.'

'How well do you know Judge Chambers?'

'I had never met him before I came here—I had never heard of him and don't know where he sat in court. I spoke to him in passing here but he kept very much to himself.

'I doubt if any of the others knew him very well.'

'We are assuming that the motive for this assault has nothing to do with a robbery, but everything to do with revenge for something for which the assailant holds a grudge—strong enough to kill—we still don't know whether the judge will pull through.'

The sergeant paused and looked him in the eye.

'So, you had no reason whatever to harm him? What do you know about the other three residents?

'Have you any reason to think that one of them has a motive to attack him for any reason.'

Robert shook his head.

'I've never heard anyone say anything against him or even indicate they knew of him before he came here. I can't vouch for the family spending their holiday here—I've never met them.'

The sergeant seemed to be satisfied with his answers.

'That's all for now. We shall be interviewing the others. We may not need to trouble you again, but, if you receive any information that may help us, please call.'

She passed a card to him with her number, rose and the two of them left the room.

He sat for a while considering the situation.

It was possible that someone from the hotel had attacked the Judge, which seemed very unlikely, but it could just as well be someone from the village nearby or further afield.

He would keep his eyes and ears open.

Chapter Eleven

The Judge remained in intensive care for the next four days.

The Detective Sergeant took the opportunity to interview the other residents during this time.

She sat down with Ted Brown while DC Cook took notes.

'How long have you been resident here?' she asked.

'About six months. I was a turf accountant in Bradley for about twenty years—built up my business and had a number of outlets when I retired.'

'Did you know or have any connection with Judge Chambers before you came here?'

'None at all. I've had very little contact with him here. He keeps himself very much to himself.'

Jennifer Ruddock looked him directly in the eye— a somewhat piercing gaze,

'Do you ever go walking on the beach in the mornings?'

Ted shook his head.

'That's not my thing—exercise.'

'Can you tell us where you were when you learned the Judge had been attacked?'

'I was in my room—it was after breakfast. I was reading my morning paper.'

That seemed to be that, and the Detective Sergeant moved on to interview the two ladies.

They found Edith Noble sitting quietly knitting.

Bearing in mind her age, there seemed to be little mileage in quizzing her.

They moved upstairs to have a word with Rose Staples.

Having knocked twice on her door, they had to wait a couple of minutes before she appeared.

They gained the impression that they were not welcome.

She told them that she had been in her room when the news of Judge Chambers reached her.

She normally had very little contact with him and had never met or had any contact with him before he arrived at the hotel.

Finally, they spoke to the family staying for a week, who were very frustrated that they could not go out and enjoy their holiday.

They expressed surprise that anyone should suspect that they would be guilty of violence.

With two young children clinging to them, there seemed little point in wasting any more time.

They had warned everyone that, depending on the evidence, they would be required to give DNA samples.

At that point, they left the hotel and drove back to the station.

Meanwhile, Robert had decided to check with the hospital every morning on the Judge's condition.

He was relieved to learn on the fifth day that the Judge has been moved to a normal bed, although he was still on the danger list.

He felt that the key to the identity of the assailant lay somewhere in the Judge's past.

On the sixth day, he decided to take a chance and drove to the hospital.

On arrival, he found that there was a police presence—a young constable was stationed outside the ward containing the Judge and three other patients.

He had decided to do the traditional thing and bring along some grapes—he knew that hospitals rarely welcomed flowers.

He spoke to the ward sister explaining who he was.

She was hesitant that his visit would be allowed— the police were keeping a vigil to ensure that no further attempt was made on the Judge's life.

The constable spoke on his phone to Detective Sergeant Ruddock.

She was not best pleased that Robert had turned up without consulting her, but, with some reluctance, allowed the visit on compassionate grounds.

The ward sister took him to one side.

'He is still very unwell. Don't stay too long. He gets very tired.'

The Judge was propped up on his bed staring ahead.

Robert approached slowly and pulled up a chair by the bed.

'Do you know who I am?' he asked quietly.

The Judge turned to him and smiled.

'Aren't you Robert Granger—from the hotel?'

Robert produced the bag of grapes.

'I don't whether you will be able to eat these—but they come with best wishes for your recovery from all of us residents.'

The Judge reached out and took Robert's hand.

'I'm very grateful to you all.'

'Have you any idea who did this to you?'

The Judge beckoned Robert to come close.

'There's just one thing that sticks in my mind.'

Chapter Twelve

'Just before I was hit, I remember a voice saying, 'this is for Joe Green'. I don't know why I should remember those words.

'I've been thinking about it and I've come to the conclusion that the key to this is in one of my past cases.

'I sat in the Crown Court for years. Unlike some judges, I kept notes—my clerk, Joy Gates, who looked after me kept the records.

'One of the reasons is that I kept seeing the same criminals appearing before me when I felt I had only just sent them down.

'I suppose that was because of remission for guilty pleas and parole.

'I think Joy is still there at Bradley Crown Court.

'Do you think you could have a word with her?'

He paused and leaned back on his pillows, looking very tired.

'Of course—if it will help to track down who did this to you.'

Robert noticed that the ward sister was watching them closely and was now shaking her head.

She came up to the bed.

'I think that's enough for now. He needs to sleep.'

Robert took the Judge's hand and gave it a slight sake.

'I'll follow this up—don't you worry.'

He left the ward with a nod to the constable who had been keeping an eye on him.

Robert saw him making a call—presumably to Detective Sergeant Ruddock to tell him he was leaving.

When he arrived back at the hotel, he looked up the number for Bradley Crown Court on his phone.

He got through to reception and asked to speak to Joy Gates.

'She is in with the Judge at the moment. Can I ask who is calling?'

'Tell her it's Robert Granger ringing on behalf of Judge Percy Chambers. I think she will want to speak with me.'

He hung on and, presently, a quiet voice came on the phone.

'This is Joy Gates—who are you exactly?'

'I've come from seeing Judge Chambers. I assume you know what happened to him?'

'I was very shocked. I was meaning to see him but is he still in hospital?'

'He's pulling round. He suggested that I see you. Apparently, he took notes about his cases and you kept them for him.'

'That's right. Obviously, I will help in any way I can. Could you come over at the end of the court day tomorrow—about five? Just ask for me at the desk.'

It was a twenty-minute drive over to Bradley—a sprawling town with little architectural merit.

The Crown Court was in an old Victorian building, very gloomy looking and hardly likely to instil confidence in anyone having to appear there.

He arrived just after five and found the receptionist about to leave for the day.

She made a call and the tiny figure of Joy Gates emerged from the depths of the building.

'I hope I can help you. I've got out the notes from the years I looked after Judge Chambers.'

She led him down a rather dark passageway into an anteroom to the court.

She had gathered together a pile of notebooks.

'What exactly are we looking for?'

Chapter Thirteen

'Just before he was attacked, he remembers someone saying, 'this is for Joe Green'.'

'So, you think this may be all about what happened to him—someone sentenced by Judge Chambers?'

'I think that's the logical conclusion—but isn't it like looking for a needle in a haystack?'

'I'll give it a try. You know, that name rings a bell from somewhere. I kept these notes in alphabetical order—Green- Green.'

She pulled out an index and started to turn through it.

Suddenly she gave a start of recognition.

'Green—I remember this now—about seven years ago. It's all coming back.

'This man Green—he was accused of seriously sexually assaulting his ten-year-old nephew.

'He denied it and said it was down to a neighbour who used to babysit for them.

'The jury asked a lot of questions—they seemed unsure—but I remember, the Judge was quite convinced of his guilt.

'When it came to summing up, he used all his skill to hint which way the verdict should go.

'The jury found him guilty—and Judge Chambers laid it on thick—gave him twelve years.'

'So, he'll still be languishing in prison now.'

Joy Gates nodded.

'Not much chance of parole for an offender like that.'

This must be the link—Robert was sure of it now.

Someone close to Joe Green was seeking to pay back the Judge for that verdict and that sentence.

He thanked Joy for her help and drove back to the hotel, deep in thought.

Whoever it was that had attacked the Judge must have known where to find him.

It was seven years later, and the assailant had not only done his homework but must have known where to find the Judge at a particular time.

It was possible, of course, that someone living locally had discovered the judge's whereabouts by accident and decided to strike.

It was obviously risky to attack him on the beach where witnesses could be about.

Robert decided to adopt the principle used by Sherlock Holmes;

Start by ruling out all the possible but unlikely alternatives until you hone in on the logical and obvious answer.

The starting point was logically someone who, at the time of Joe Green's trial, was living in Bradley.

That narrowed down the field.

Who then was able to follow the Judge on foot, strike the deadly blow and get away before Robert had finished his swim and turned back to the beach?

There was only one person that he knew who had lived and worked in Bradley, who knew the Judge's habits and was able-bodied enough to strike and disappear.

The man who professed to take no exercise—which nicely deflected suspicion elsewhere.

That man—Robert decided—could only be Ted Brown.

Chapter Thirteen

Robert was sitting in his hotel suite.

He now had the obvious suspect in his sights.

The police were only at the start of their investigations and might never make the connection with Joe Green.

The fact that they had placed a PC on guard in the ward indicated that they were aware of the serious risk that the Judge's attacker—who had intended to kill—might well now decide to finish the job.

At breakfast the following day, Richard was chatting amiably with Ted Brown as usual.

'Are the police making any progress?' asked Ted.

'I don't know about that but when I visited the Judge he told me that, just before he was hit, someone said, 'this is for Joe Green'.

'He remembers now that he sentenced a Joe Green some years ago and he is wondering whether that is the connection. Perhaps someone close to Joe Green was looking for revenge.'

Robert noticed a slight reaction from Ted.

'Has he told the police about this yet?'

'Not yet, but they are coming to see him tomorrow morning when they think he will be fit to be interviewed again.

'Once they know about the Joe Green connection, it can't be long before they put two and two together and narrow the field of suspects.'

Ted had now gone noticeably quiet.

He got up suddenly from the table and left the room.

Robert had laid the bait and now all he had to do was wait to see what Ted would do.

He had been daring enough to attack the Judge on the beach knowing that Robert was nearby.

He would know that, once the police spoke to the Judge again, it would not be long before they found the connection.

If he had really intended to kill the Judge, he would not hesitate to finish the job now.

It was highly unlikely that he would attempt anything during the day.

The residents kept their private cars at the rear of the hotel.

Robert knew that Ted drove a BMW with a highly personalised design, of which he was very proud.

It was a long day as Robert kept a quiet eye on the car park.

Should he contact Jennifer Ruddock and put her in the picture?

He decided not at this stage—after all, he had got this far on his own and he wanted to see it out.

Darkness fell and there was still no sign of Ted.

By one o'clock he was beginning to feel drowsy when he spotted Ted moving stealthily towards his car.

If he was heading to the hospital, Robert would have no difficulty following at a discreet distance.

The BMW moved slowly from the car park onto the adjacent road.

Robert watched its tail lights disappear and then started to follow.

There was little traffic about and he had to keep well back to avoid being spotted.

Now he felt he could contact Jennifer Ruddock and ask for back-up.

She answered after three rings—he managed to summarise the events of the past two days.

All she really wanted to know was that he was following a suspect heading for the hospital in the middle of the night—and well aware that they had recently removed the Judge's police protection.

As he reached the hospital car park, he spotted Ted's vehicle parked up and saw him approaching the entrance.

He followed but then lost sight of him as he approached the reception desk where one sleepy nurse was on duty.

Somehow Ted had slipped past without being seen.

It was not a large hospital and it would not take him long to track down the Judge.

At least Robert had the drop on him as he knew precisely where to go.

He reached the ward and peered in anxiously.

All the patients were asleep—there was no sign of Ted.

He was about to turn when he felt something sharp against his neck.

'Don't move—I don't want to do this but I won't hesitate'.

Robert kept completely still.

'So, tell me, Ted—what was the connection with Joe Green?'

He felt the blade pressing into his neck.

'He's my brother. That Judge never gave him a chance—decided he was guilty from day one—fair trial—you must be joking! He told the jury to convict. Then he piled on the sentence. He deserved to die.'

'What are you going to do now? Are you going to kill me and the Judge?'

Suddenly a voice rang out!

'Put the knife down-'

Jennifer Ruddock appeared from the gloom with two armed officers.

Ted never knew what hit him—he was on the floor in a flash and into handcuffs.

Chapter Fifteen

Robert was back to his peaceful existence again.

The two women residents now greeted him with a little more respect. To Jean-Claude he was a hero—he had obviously spun them a colourful story.

Jennifer Ruddock paid him the compliment of coming alone to the hotel for a de-briefing.

The police normally hated civilians like Robert—especially retired professionals—beating them to the punch.

This seemed to be an exception.

She positively glowed with praise for him.

'When you are off duty, would you care to go for a drink sometime?'

She smiled.

'I thought you would never ask.'

THE END

Paradise Postponed

Chapter One

'Someone has been asking after you,' said Jean-Claude casually as he brought in breakfast.

'Male or female?'

'Male—and would not give me a name which made me rather suspicious. You know how I protect the privacy of my guests.'

Robert Granger pulled a face.

'Don't like the sound of it—where is he now?'

'It was on the phone. He seemed to be pretty sure that you were here. I didn't give you away.'

'So, he could be anywhere—lurking outside.'

He got up, reluctantly leaving the egg and bacon generously spread across his plate.

Jean-Claude had rapidly accustomed himself to British tastes after leaving the rarefied delights of French cuisine.

Robert was well aware that it was probably doing nothing for his waistline.

There was no one else in the breakfast room at the moment.

He walked cautiously to one of the windows giving him a wide sweep of the lawn and garden.

No one was there except Sam, the gardener, yawning as he pushed a wheelbarrow.

Robert moved to a side window, giving him a clear view of the drive and front of the hotel.

He could see further down the road and noted that a black car with shaded windows was parked in a prime position to note any comings and goings.

He felt a prickling in his scalp—something told him that whoever was parked out there was waiting for him to emerge.

In a flash, he thought back to all the many errant husbands he had tracked down for cheated wives, and the various confrontations that had sometimes been unavoidable.

There had been plenty of threats, most of which he had brushed off at the time, but one or two vindictive cheating husbands had promised reprisals.

He knew that memories were funny things—some people harboured grudges for years.

It had always been his policy to face things rather than try to run away.

Short of slipping round the back and clambering over an overgrown eight-feet-high wall, he could only come and go through the front entrance.

'Sod them,' he decided, 'Whoever is out there is just going to have to wait for me to finish my breakfast.'.

He returned to the table, tucked into his bacon and egg and buttered a couple of slices of toast.

Jean-Claude was a master coffee blender and he drained his cup to the last dregs.

After twenty minutes or so, he returned to the window and noted that the black car was still in situ.

'It's now or never,' he said to himself, crossing the spacious hall and opening the front door.

It was impossible, as he crossed the road, to see who was sitting in the car.

He approached the driver's door, trying to look brisk and business-like, and tapped on the window.

After a few moments, the window slightly lowered, to reveal a chauffeur in a peaked cap at the wheel.

He could see in the back seat an old lady, very well dressed, with a large, obviously expensive, handbag on her lap.

She leaned forward slightly.

'I take it you are Robert Granger—lately a private detective?'

He nodded, completely taken aback.

'My name is Gladys Forsyth. No doubt you have heard of me. We have never met but your reputation goes before you.

'I have a mission for you. I think you will find it not uninteresting—and rewarding.'

The chauffeur suddenly opened his door and moved effortlessly behind Robert to hold open the back door of the car.

'If you would like to get in, I will explain.'

Chapter Two

Robert felt surprised and very flattered to be approached by someone so august as Gladys Forsyth.

The very wealthy widow of Richard Forsyth, the shipping magnate, had in the past attracted lots of column inches in the press for her expensive tastes.

Now in her seventies, but as feisty as ever, she lived in luxury with a younger partner.

Quite where she had heard of Robert, was a mystery to him.

'You are obviously wondering why I would single you out,' she said with a smile.

'Let us just say that you sorted out a rather tangled mess for one of my old friends. She passed me your name and you come highly recommended.'

'It must have been some time ago,' Robert replied, 'Because I have been officially retired for the last few years.'

Gladys stretched out her heavily bejewelled hand and placed it on his.

'The task I have in mind will, I hope, rekindle your interest and, if you are successful, I don't think you would have to worry about your finances again.'

'You are making it very hard to refuse.'

'So I have your attention then?' she enquired.

She had removed her hand and was now giving him a rather piercing gaze, visible even in the rather dingy confines of the limousine.

'I can make no promises until I hear your proposition,' said Robert. 'You have to bear in mind that I am very happy and settled in my new life here.'

Gladys looked across at the hotel rather sniffily.

'I can't believe at your age that you have settled for retirement. You are obviously still fit and active.

'I assessed that as you were crossing to the car. I also read that you were recently instrumental in bringing a serious criminal to justice.'

Robert shrugged.

'That's true—but the case rather fell into my lap. I can't really take much credit for it.'

Gladys shook her head.

'Don't undersell yourself. You are a much rarer animal than you realise.

'Now—do you want to hear my proposition or not?'

'Yes, go ahead Do you mind if I record our conversation on the phone?'

'I have no objection so long as you keep the contents strictly confidential.'

'Of course.'

Gladys now reached forward and pressed a button, which resulted in a glass screen coming down between the front and rear of the car.

'A little background to assist you. For some years, I brought up my young niece, Jenny, and my nephew, Tom. My sister—their mother—had died young and I felt an obligation to take over their upbringing and education.

'They grew up and left me about five years ago. I tried to keep in touch but, eventually, they dropped out of my life.

'I have no idea of their whereabouts. All I know is that Jenny is a talented dress designer and Tom was interested in hotel management.

'To put it bluntly, I have lived a very full life but it has taken its toll on my health.

'I would like to include them in my will but, for that, I need to track them down.

'Will you help me?'

'I will certainly try.'

Gladys sighed with relief.

'You will receive ten thousand up front—for your services—and a generous spending allowance.

'I will put you in touch with my accountant who will sort out the details.

'Just one condition: you are to report to me and to me alone on your progress—do you understand?'

Chapter Three

Early the following morning, Robert received a call from Hector Norwich, who announced himself importantly as Gladys Forsyth's accountant.

'The persons you are being asked to trace are Jenny Holgate and Tom Nugent.

'I have their last known addresses for you. I am sending you a photo of each of them—I am not sure how much help they will be as they were taken some years ago.

'Of course, either of them could have changed their appearance in the meantime—or even their identity.

'If you will give me details of your bank account, I will transfer ten thousand pounds—I think that was the agreed sum—and a further two thousand for expenses at this stage.

'Let me know when you need more—I will need proper receipts, of course—but there is no limit.

'Mrs Forsyth has indicated that she will pay whatever it takes. That is, of course, entirely her decision.'

In other words, he was not happy to be giving Robert what amounted to an open chequebook.

After the call, Robert sat with his morning coffee and took stock.

If indeed Gladys Forsyth was asking him to pursue this enquiry out of the goodness of her heart—and she was not actually renowned for her generosity—why would Hector Norwich even suggest that Jenny and Tom might have changed their appearance or identity?

Of course, he had no idea on what sort of terms the parties had separated or why indeed either Jenny or Tom had wanted to sever relations with her.

There had been no suggestion by Gladys that either of them had wanted to disappear—families sometimes lost touch and that was just the way it was.

Nevertheless, it had very much increased the possible difficulties ahead of him if it were true that they were deliberately avoiding any contact with their esteemed aunt.

The money duly arrived as promised, together with a couple of rather ancient photos.

Jenny had been snapped on some sort of continental holiday, smiling at the camera in a bathing costume. She looked about eighteen.

Tom had been filmed at some function where he was wearing a dinner jacket.

Jenny had long fair hair and was a pretty girl. Tom was dark, tall and really rather striking.

Obviously, these shots had been taken at least twenty years ago, since Robert guessed that, bearing in mind Gladys's age which was well known from her publicity, both Jenny and Tom would in all likelihood be in their early forties.

So, a great deal of water had passed under the bridge in that time.

If indeed either or both of them were still living and working in the UK, they could be anywhere.

The clues that Gladys had given him—Jenny's interest in dress design and Tom in hotel management—were at least a start.

He decided to begin with Jenny.

The internet was full of famous fashion houses—perhaps one of them had either employed or at least knew of Jenny Holgate.

He rang around half a dozen, drawing a blank, but then received a possible lead from one of the London fashion houses.

'We did have a Jenny working here a couple of years ago—but not Holgate. I can't remember her surname.'

'Do you mind if I come and see you? I have some identification which could help but would prefer to discuss it personally.'

She seemed surprised but delighted that anyone would take the trouble to trek into London from the Isle of Wight.

They fixed an appointment and Robert crossed by ferry and then travelled up by train—first class.

It was a long time since he had allowed himself that luxury—but why not?

The fashion house was in Chelsea, and the taxi dropped him off right outside.

He felt completely out of his comfort zone as he entered the frightfully smart premises, where amazingly-dressed young women were dashing about.

Dora Haines suddenly materialised from the inner sanctum and came up to him, stretching out a languorous hand.

She had deep blue hair, wearing plenty of make-up and eye shadow.

She was probably in her mid-thirties and full of confidence, which Robert found was seeping away by the minute.

'Mr Granger?' she enquired. 'I'm flattered that you have come all the way from—where is it—the Isle of Wight?'

She made a vague gesture which, to Robert, indicated that she had only the sketchiest idea where that was.

'Come up to my office on the first floor and we'll have a little talk. Coffee or something stronger?'

'A black coffee would be fine.'

'Then come along and I'll see if we can help you.'

Chapter Four

Once they were settled upstairs with their coffees, Dora consulted her phone.

She scrutinised details of the various assistants in the fashion house over the past few years.

It was obvious that there had been a lot of comings and goings by personnel.

'It's quite hard to keep track of them all,' said Dora.

'I do remember a Jenny—but not Holgate—she was called Rossiter.'

'I have an old photo,' said Robert, fishing it out.

'Taken some twenty years ago—I hope it helps.'

Dora stared at it intensely.

'I remember that hair—and her face seems familiar. I'm sure that's Jenny Rossiter.'

'Do you know what happened to her? I suppose it's a long shot.'

Dora now looked pleased with herself.

'What I do remember is that she liked to help out in a café—in her spare time, which wasn't much as we are rather slave drivers here.'

She gave a sort of guttural laugh and took a swig of coffee.

'It was somewhere on Exmoor. A little village—she loved it there. Dulverton—that's it.'

Robert thanked her and prepared to go on his way.

'You must be very keen—a missing relative?'

'Something like that. Well, thank you for the information—and the coffee.'

Robert decided to cut short the visit. He did not wish to disclose any more information.

As he stepped back into the street, his sixth sense told him that someone somewhere was watching.

He set out to find a taxi, carefully checking the area.

About fifty metres away, a man of about forty, casually dressed, was standing looking at his phone.

He seemed strangely familiar.

Then Robert realised that he had seen him before—in the corridor of the train as he was looking for a compartment.

They had actually passed, with Robert excusing himself for compelling the man to squeeze back to allow him to go by.

It was too much of a coincidence to ignore.

It suddenly occurred to him that perhaps he had been followed right from the island.

A couple of taxis cruised by before he was able to hail one.

The man had moved and was also in the process of waving down a taxi.

It was now a question of finding a suitable train from Paddington.

He figured on his phone that the nearest station was probably Exeter.

On the platform, he placed himself back from the destination board, having booked a one-way ticket.

All the time for the next thirty minutes, he kept a wary eye for the man following but there was no sign.

Robert figured he was a professional, which disturbed him.

There was a two-hour wait for the train and he moved away to a restaurant and gave himself a good meal.

It was crowded with fellow travellers but still no sign of anyone following.

He waited, as the train pulled into the station, to the very last minute to allow all the passengers to alight, before moving swiftly up the platform and entering a carriage.

He quickly glanced out before settling to scan the area, but still no sign of anyone following.

Perhaps he had been wrong—but he didn't think so.

Chapter Five

It was a high-speed train and seemed to be in Exeter before he expected it.

Now he was faced with the logistical problem of travelling up into Exmoor.

Given his lavish expenses, he had no hesitation in finding the nearest taxi and setting off up the Exe Valley.

There had been quite an exodus at the station; he had not hung about to see whether anyone was on his tail.

He sat with the driver—a jolly local sort who was obviously intrigued by his reasons for the journey, but Robert contented himself with some general chat and gave nothing away.

The day was fine and the scenery splendid.

They turned into the high street of Dulverton and Robert excused himself, paid the driver and took stock.

There were obviously cafés in the town and there was nothing for it but to trawl them with the photo of Jenny.

At the third attempt, having sat and ordered his third cup of tea of the afternoon, he was rewarded.

'I'm sure that's Jenny,' said the proprietress, sitting down heavily opposite him.

'She used to come down at weekends and help us out. Always glad to get out of London. Sometimes met a young man—I think he was her brother. He gave us a hand washing up.'

'How long ago was this?'

She hesitated, wondering for the first time why a stranger would be asking these questions.

Robert could sense her native caution.

'I'm trying to trace them. They've inherited some money.'

He decided not to elaborate—that would probably be a reasonable explanation.

'Oh, I see. Well, all I can tell you is that they suddenly stopped coming about a year ago.

'No explanation. Jess, in the kitchen, heard them talking one day about his running a small hotel somewhere on the coast.

'I can't remember where—it was Combe or something. But everything ends with Combe up there.'

'That's very helpful.'

She seemed pleased to have helped, and he was now faced with another cross-country journey.

It was late afternoon, and the last thing he wanted was to be stranded somewhere on the north Devon coast with night falling.

'Is there such a thing as a taxi nearby?' he asked.

'Just down the high street—you'll see it advertised in the window.'

He wandered off looking for a newsagent where he could buy a detailed map of the coast.

An old-fashioned approach, but there was nothing likely to be more helpful.

There were few pedestrians about but, as he walked along, his sixth sense kicked in again.

He was certain someone was watching him.

He decided to contact Gladys and give her a progress report.

'Where are you?' she enquired.

'In a little town in Exmoor. I think I am making real progress.'

'You haven't found them yet?'

'I'm well on the trail. Should have more news for you in a day or two.'

He rang off, spotting a newspaper rack sitting outside a shop.

He was gratified to find that the shop had numerous maps, including a detailed large-scale view of the north coast from Barnstable to Minehead.

Chapter Six

Robert felt that he had no option but to return to the café and see if he could find Jess still working in the kitchen.

He found the lad toiling away at the sink, clearing the afternoon's debris.

It was hard to attract his attention with all the noise, but Robert managed to pin him down at least to the approximate area of coast where Tom had operated.

It was an enormous sweep of coastline from Barnstaple to Minehead, with hundreds of inlets and bays.

'The small hotel which he managed—the location ended with a 'combe', didn't it? Do you know that coast?'

Jess paused a moment and put down his dishcloth.

'I lived up there for a while—I think he mentioned Diracombe. It's off the main coast road about a couple of miles—down a narrow track to the sea.

'The hotel is perched on a cliff—a very steep drive up to it but with a great view.'.

'Is it open all year?'

'I think so. It's a meeting place for bird watchers so it's generally busy.'

Robert thanked him profusely and left him to return to his duties.

With the evening drawing on, he needed somewhere to stay overnight.

He took potluck with a guest house down the street and settled in for an early night.

The following morning, he was up early and was gratified that he was offered a full English breakfast cooked to perfection.

The owner was kind enough to book him a taxi for his journey north, and he set off with a degree of optimism.

Jess was certainly true to his word—once having left the main road, the narrow twisty lane, bounded on each side by traditional high hedges, provided no view ahead.

Each sharp corner provided a challenge for a driver with no view—anything could be coming the other way and there was never room to pass.

They had one hairy moment with a milk float but it squeezed past and, after a few minutes, the lane rose steeply up to an entrance gate announcing, 'High Point Hotel'.

An imposing granite building loomed up as they drove into the yard.

It was a clear morning and, as he got out, Robert was met with a magnificent sweeping view along the coast from above the cliffs.

The taxi driver was anxious to get back, so Robert paid him with a sizeable tip and entered the hotel.

For a moment he imagined that he would be faced with the elusive Tom, but, instead, a very fit-looking blonde lady emerged from a side door and greeted him.

This was certainly not Jenny unless she had shed at least a dozen years.

'Can I help you?' she ventured, noting that Robert was unable to hide his disappointment.

'I was looking for Tom Nugent—I understood that he was manager here'.

She shook her head.

'I'm afraid you're too late. Tom was manager here before me. He left suddenly about six months ago.'

'Did his sister, Jenny, live here by any chance?'

'For a few weeks then they left together. Things were not going well and perhaps it was for the best.

'I don't want to be too critical—this place is not the easiest to manage—we are in the eye of the winter storms and there is perpetual damage caused by the weather.'

Robert decided to come straight to the point.

'I was hoping to trace them—.they have inherited a considerable legacy. I've been sent by the lawyers.'

'I'm sorry it has proved a wild goose chase.'

'Do you have any idea where they went?'

'I don't suppose they would mind my letting you know in the circumstances. They asked me to redirect their post to the Isles of Scilly.

'Apparently, they have rented a cottage on one of the out islands—St Agnes.'

Chapter Seven

Robert had holidayed on the Isles of Scilly once and had a fair idea where St Agnes was situated as the most westerly of the small island group.

He now felt that the net was finally closing in on Tom and Jenny, but before he planned his strategy he decided to report to base once again.

After a while, he found Gladys entertaining friends in one of her favourite cafés – the noise in the background was deafening.

'I think I have found them,' he announced over the din.

'Well done. I assume you are keeping your head well down and not giving the game away to either of them.'

'I am in a small hotel in Devon—they have long departed from here to a cottage on St Agnes in the Isles of Scilly.'

'I have no idea where that is but I assume you will be on your way there.'

'I will have to arrange a flight over to the islands but I'll report when I get there.'

Gladys seemed to be satisfied and clearly anxious to get back to her friends.

Robert investigated the possibility of flights from Land's End to St Mary's—the holiday season was over and the flights less frequent, but he found one for later in the day, provided he could get there by taxi from the hotel.

The flight by light plane across to the islands is always an experience—as the cliffs beyond Land's End give way to the open sea, with the anticipation of seeing the Eastern Isles (the easternmost point of the Scillies) coming into view a few minutes later.

There were only eight passengers on the flight.

They landed on St Mary's in bright sunlight, and he soon found himself deposited in the town centre.

Robert decided to indulge in a coffee before heading for the quay where he would find an afternoon boat across to St Agnes.

It was one of the older boats, quite low in the water, and he noted there was a swell on the sea and a sharp wind.

He remembered that the crossing to St Agnes could be quite rough, with the boats taking on water from the higher waves.

The crossing was no more than twenty minutes and a number of hardy souls huddled in groups.

Robert felt that he was rather lightly dressed for the occasion and was chilled by the time the boat moored alongside the jetty at St Agnes.

The question now was whether or not he should identify himself.

The way Gladys had warned him to keep his head down seemed to indicate that, while she was keen to learn the whereabouts of Tom and Jenny, she was not keen for them to know she had sent him to find them.

On the other hand, he had to be sure who they were.

He decided that the best way to start was to drop into the Turk's Head above the quay and make enquiries there.

He entered the bar and ordered a pint of local brew.

'Do you happen to know where I can find Tom Nugent?' he asked innocently.

The barman looked at him quizzically.

'Funny—you're the second person who has asked that. Tom must be having a party.'

He smiled to himself.

'Take the road up into the island, past the local stores on your left and beyond the coastguard cottages—you'll find the cottage set back down a track about fifty metres from the road.

'You'll see a café sign outside—but they're shut now.'

Robert thanked him, downed his pint, and set off as advised.

There was no traffic on the island apart from tractors moving produce about.

He had to skip into the hedge a couple of times as they bounded past him along the narrow road.

Following directions, he easily identified the solid granite coastguard cottages and spotted the track leading off to the left.

A single-storey cottage came into view ahead.

He approached very quietly—there was no movement anywhere.

Chapter Eight

Robert moved with infinite caution towards what he took to be the front door of the cottage.

He could see that this was wide open.

As he reached the door he knocked a few times— no response.

He then called out a couple of times but, again, no answer.

There was a man's bicycle parked outside.

He decided that it could do no harm to enter the cottage and he could make some excuse if he disturbed someone there.

The sitting room was rather dingy and dark with old furniture, a table and chairs; untidy and cluttered.

He called out again, and this time heard a faint whimpering coming from the next room.

He decided it could be some animal—perhaps a dog tied up somewhere.

Moving cautiously, he heard the whimpering sound again, louder than before.

There was a small dining area beyond the sitting room and, as he entered and accustomed his eyes, he saw a man slumped against the wall.

As he approached, the man whimpered again and Robert could see that he was bleeding profusely from the face.

His wrists and ankles were roughly tied.

Bending over to examine him, Robert realised that he was barely conscious.

'Is it you, Tom?' he whispered.

The man looked up and appeared relieved to see Robert.

'I didn't tell him. I didn't tell him. He's gone to find Jenny—but he's coming back.'

'Where has she gone?'

'To the village shop—I was afraid he might run into her on the way back. You've got to find her and warn her. There's a way back here behind the lighthouse.'

Robert quickly untied him and helped him stand up with difficulty.

'He caught me by surprise. Was on me before I could do anything.'

Robert helped him slowly into the sitting room to a chair.

'I'll get you some water. Stay there and I'll go and find Jenny.'

Robert realised now that he was right—he had been followed and whoever was on his trail had been tipped off by Gladys after his last call to her.

Somehow he had arrived on an earlier flight and caught the earlier boat.

Now it was vital to find Jenny before she was harmed.

He left Tom and set off at a good pace back down the road.

The problem was that he had no idea of the identity of the assailant.

He could be any one of the men who passed him by.

It took him five minutes to reach the local shop—and the first piece of luck today—he saw emerging with a large basket, a person who could only be Jenny—she still had the long fair hair from her young photo.

'You're Jenny,' he blurted out, realising that she would not have the faintest notion who he was.

She gave him a bemused smile.

'Do I know you?' she asked.

'There's no time for me to explain. Your brother has been badly hurt—I've just come from your cottage. He said there's a back way without going up the road.'

Jenny was still trying to take this all in.

'Yes—there is.'

'I don't think it's safe to go back by the road. Will you lead me and I'll explain everything?'

Chapter Nine

They set off at a good pace, Jenny leading the way across a rough pebbly track.

At intervals, they could glimpse the sparkling sea in the distance.

'I had better start,' said Robert, rather out of breath.

'Your Aunt Gladys sent me to find you both. I'm a private detective—retired but brought back for this one job. The way she put it to me was that she wished to include you in her will but had lost touch.'

Jenny paused to let out a loud laugh.

'Fat chance of that,' she said.

'I'd better come clean and tell you the whole story. Our mother died quite young and Gladys took us on— well, she gave us a home but she treated us like slaves— and forced us to do everything for her.

'This got worse as we grew up. All right, she had everything and we were penniless but the moment we could escape we got out.

'She tried hard to keep tabs on us, so we had to keep moving.'

'Yes—I've seen plenty of evidence of that.'

They pushed through a thick hedge, trying to avoid stinging nettles.

'Now comes the confession. Gladys had inherited some really valuable paintings—I mean worth millions. They were kept in a locked room below the house but Tom was clever and found a way of getting in.

'Gladys had no interest in art—only money, so she rarely went down to view them.

'As a parting shot, Tom managed to smuggle out a painting—French impressionist—worth a fortune.

'We realised that one day she would discover it missing and put two and two together.

'Obviously, that day has come and she is now determined to get it back.'

'So what she told me was a load of rubbish.'

'Absolutely—she wants the painting back—that's why she instructed you.'

Robert took her arm.

'Stop a minute. It's not so simple as that. Gladys has had me followed—every inch of the way.

'She's simply been using me as a means to an end.

'Someone dangerous has followed me and somehow got ahead of me at the last minute.

'He must have caught your brother off guard. I found him in the cottage in a poor state.

'He kept saying, 'I didn't tell him'—now I realise that he was referring to the location of the painting.'

They pressed on up the track—the back of the cottage was now clearly visible.

'We keep it well hidden,' said Jenny. 'No one would ever find it without us.'

'You mean that you have it here—on the island?'

'When we took the cottage we took a good look round. We suspected there might be a cellar of some sort, but it took us a long time to find out how to get in.

'The painting is well-secured down there. It's safer now than at any time as we have moved around.'

Robert stopped and motioned Jenny to a standstill.

'You have to face the fact that Gladys will know for certain where you are and that you have the painting. What do you intend to do?'

'Let's sort this fellow out first—then we'll discuss it.'

As they approached the cottage, there was no sign of movement.

'You keep well out of sight and leave me to deal with this,' said Robert.

He entered the cottage silently, motioning Tom to silence—he was still barely conscious.

He hid behind the front door, waiting.

After a few minutes, there was the unmistakable sound of feet approaching.

They paused for a moment outside the door—and evidently concluding that all was well, the feet moved on and into the doorway.

Robert appeared, the figure was largely in shadow, but he provided a suitable target.

A swift low kick—the man doubled over and Robert caught him with a clean blow in the face.

It was all over—there was no fight left in him—Robert leaned over and administered the coup de grace blow to the jaw.

'You can come in now!' he shouted, as Jenny rushed up to inspect the damage.

'I think you have a resident sergeant of police on St Mary's,' said Robert, 'Perhaps you would give him a call and inform him that there has been a violent incident which I am sure he would like to deal with urgently—and discreetly.'

Chapter Ten

They left it until the following day.

Robert knew that Gladys would be on tenterhooks not having heard from the 'hitman' or Robert.

It would do her no harm to be kept in suspense.

By mid-morning they could not contain themselves.

Tom had pulled round, bathed his wounds and was raring to go.

Robert put in the call.

It appeared from the splashing that they had caught Gladys in the bath—luxuriating, no doubt.

'I thought you ought to know that I am here on the island with Tom and Jenny—and the local police.

'You didn't tell me that you were having me followed. Unfortunately, he got to Tom and assaulted him—the police are dealing with that.

'Jenny would like to discuss the question of the painting.

'It is quite secure and well-hidden.

'She would like to do a deal.'

'I want that painting back—they stole it.'

'I'm afraid there is a price to pay for that.'

'I don't negotiate with people. She'll have to talk to Hector Norwich.'

She ended the call.

'If I were you I'd wait an hour or two and then ring Norwich,' Robert suggested.

They went out for a drink and came back about midday.

Jenny put through the call and Norwich answered immediately.

'Mrs Forsyth understands that you want to do business.'

'Yes,' said Jenny. 'We have the painting—she wants it back. I understand it is worth millions; she would not miss giving us a suitable settlement for its return.'

'Name your figure.'

'A payment of a hundred thousand to each of us with no strings attached—when the money is in our bank, we will return the painting personally.'

There was an intake of breath at the other end.

He rang off.

An hour later, Norwich rang back.

He spoke only three words, 'It's a deal.'

A few days later, Robert received a call from Gladys.

'I apologise for wrong-footing you, Mr Granger—I don't want you to think badly of me—I only wanted back what was mine.'

'I understand—and I think I have been more than well paid upfront. Forget expenses.'

THE END

Paradise Predicted

Chapter One

'Jean-Claude, would you mind making me one of your famous packed lunches today?'

'You're not here for lunch, Mr Granger?'

'No, I'm going to find a nice spot on the coast and take a long walk.'

Robert never needed to ask what was in the lunches that Jean-Claude put together—they were always delicious and he liked to give himself a surprise.

The summer of his third year of retirement in the hotel was rapidly drawing to an end.

There had already been hints of the chill of impending autumn, and the wind could be cutting at the coast—particularly in the early mornings.

Breakfast was over and he was now in his suite on the first floor, surveying the sweeping view from his balcony.

The memory of his adventures on the Isles of Scilly was fast fading.

Retirement had its merits, of course, and he wanted for nothing materially, but the hankering to get his teeth into something never entirely faded.

He had begun to plan his day when the unexpected happened.

Mrs Rose Staples, the highly dignified old lady who occupied the next-door suite, rarely spoke, save to nod when they passed on the stairs, and she rarely appeared in the dining room, taking all her meals alone.

Robert had no idea as to her background—he assumed she was a widow and obviously had private means of some sort.

She seemed well-bred and was very aloof, treating all those she met with a quiet but certain disdain.

It was, therefore, something of a shock when there was a sharp knock at his door.

Even more so when he found Mrs Staples standing there in a state of some distress.

'May I come in and sit down—it is Mr Granger, isn't it? I'm sorry that we have not been properly introduced—entirely my fault, I'm afraid.'

This was such an unexpected admission that Robert was at a loss for words.

Instead, he summoned her to a comfortable chair where she sank down and stared for a few moments at the luxurious carpet.

'I don't know really where to start,' she said. 'I understand that at one time you were a private detective and carried out enquiries of a discreet nature.'

'That was my profession for a number of years. If you are looking for my help, I can only say that I have been retired for some time.'

Robert felt that nowadays it was wise to preface any involvement with a warning.

'I have been observing you since your arrival here. You sorted out the attempted murder of poor Judge Chambers—an appalling affair which shocked us all.

'At the time, I was on the point of moving—none of us felt safe here until the matter was cleared up.

'Thank goodness you were able to solve it. I must admit that I never trusted the fellow—seedy and, dare I say it, not quite the sort of person that we welcome in a hotel of this sort.'

'That's all well in the past,' Robert reassured her.

'What has made you so upset?'

Mrs Staples turned to him, making a determined effort to pull herself together.

'This is not like me at all,' she said.

'I need your help because I have been receiving some threatening messages and I don't know how to deal with them.

'I had better tell you about the trust. I am the recipient of substantial trust funds during my life. They are administered by an organisation set up by my late father and a firm of lawyers is in charge.

'I have two sisters who are younger and who are struggling financially because they were overlooked by my father when he set up the trust.

'On my death, the trust will leapfrog them in favour of several nephews and nieces who will share the spoils between them for life.

'There has been great resentment in the family and someone is trying to accelerate the day when they will inherit.

'I am of a nervous disposition and have suffered heart problems since my fifties.

'You see my dilemma.'

Robert had been listening intently.

'And you want it to stop.'

Chapter Two

'You say you have received a number of threats,' said Robert.

Mrs Staples moved to a cabinet on the far side of the room, opened it and came back with some documents.

'These have arrived at regular intervals over the past few weeks.'

She showed him three sheets of paper, on which, had been pasted messages.

The letters of the words had been clearly cut out of various periodicals, to avoid being identified.

The first read: YOU ARE A WASTE OF SPACE.

The second: TIME YOU DEPARTED THIS PLANET.

The third: HURRY UP AND DIE.

'Not too subtle hints there,' said Robert. 'How did they arrive?'

'Not through the post—someone must have delivered them at night and simply put them through the letterbox at the front of the hotel.'

'So, nobody was ever seen delivering them.'

'As you can imagine, I have kept this quiet—I did not want to draw attention to myself or make a fuss. The messages were always in a plain envelope with my name in capitals.'.

Mrs Staples was clearly becoming upset and Robert invited her to sit down.

She settled on a large comfortable settee.

'Can I get you anything—a drink?'

She shook her head and invited him to join her.

'If you are going to help me, I must give you a lot more information about the family.'

Robert had been mulling things over and decided that this was a case that was worthwhile and intriguing.

'I'll certainly do what I can, if only to stop these appalling messages.'

Mrs Staples breathed a sigh of relief.

'I'm very willing to pay you for your services,' she said.

'No, I don't want payment except to cover my expenses.'

She seemed surprised but readily agreed to his terms.

'Now, let me give you details to help you. The lawyer administering the trust is Jonathan Scott of Scott and Co.—a well-known firm in the City.

'My sisters are Jasmine, the mother of three sons David, Paul and James, and Ellen, mother of Craig and Harriet.

'I have their addresses for you. I mentioned that my sisters are struggling—I help them financially from time to time but they have never gotten over the fact that my father overlooked them in my favour.

'If I had simply been left a legacy, I guess that they would have tried to challenge it in the courts—I hear that is the popular thing these days.

'I would hate to think that they would stoop so low as to encourage these threats-'

The thought seemed to affect her and she took a flowery handkerchief and dabbed an eye.

'Do you think that either of them knows who is behind it?' asked Robert.

'Perhaps that is something you could find out. I don't want to teach you your business but that does seem, to me, a good place to start.'

Robert spent a few minutes noting the full names and addresses of the sisters, nieces and nephews.

'A couple more things,' he said, 'Do you have any instinct as to which of them is likely to be vindictive enough to threaten you and, apart from the notes, has there been any other intimidation—phone calls, for instance?'

Mrs Staples shook her head.

'I have a completely open mind—but where large sums of money are at stake, people can do unusual things.'

Chapter Three

After years of living quietly on the Isle of Wight, Robert found the prospect of travelling to the City of London rather daunting.

He imagined that he might find Jonathan Scott a rather distant prospect, but the name Rose Staples seemed to wave a magic wand.

He could see Robert the next day at eleven a.m. which would give him time to take the various trains required.

On arrival, the offices of Scott and Co. boasted a magnificent entrance and the interior would not have looked out of place in a five-star hHotel.

The receptionist greeted him cordially and whisked him in a very elegant lift to the second floor.

There, he found Jonathan Scott had been alerted to meet him and led him into a spacious and richly furnished office, where he was invited to sit before a large mahogany desk.

'So, you are representing Rose Staples.'

Jonathan looked him up and down critically.

Robert had at least made the effort to dress as smartly as he still could, having discarded his more formal attire some time ago.

'She has asked me to see you about a rather delicate matter,' Robert began.

Jonathan was all ears.

'I understand that she is the beneficiary of trust funds during her lifetime.

'She has told me that her father preferred her to her two sisters and that, when she dies, the trust will pass to various nephews and nieces.'

Jonathan was looking pensive.

'I realise that Rose has taken you into her confidence, but I don't know far I can disclose further details of the trust.

'I can however put you right about one thing. Rose has obviously misunderstood one very important element.

'When she dies, the nephews and nieces will share the spoils equally—the trust will come to an end.'

Now the threats and intimidation began to make sense.

'So, each of them stands to inherit a fortune.'

'Without disclosing any actual figures, I would say they will each inherit a million or two—even dividing the capital between the five of them.'

Robert now felt that he could be frank with Jonathan as the trustee of the fund.

'The reason I have been instructed is because Rose has been receiving some very unpleasant threats—anonymous letters which have upset and frightened her very much.

'She has asked me to try and trace their origin. From the point of view of motive, it looks very much as though one of the family is behind it—perhaps hoping to accelerate his or her inheritance.'

Jonathan shook his head.

'I simply can't believe that any of the family would stoop to such behaviour.

'I have met the two sisters who struck me as highly respectable, and the nephews and nieces all struck me—on the occasions I have met them—as well brought up and responsible.'

Robert got up to leave, not wanting to take up any more valuable earning time—certainly not at top city lawyers' hourly rates.

'It is kind of you to see me,' he said. 'It is not a pleasant task but somebody is behind this and I must do my best to find out who as soon as possible.

'If Mrs Staples receives any more of these messages, she may be severely upset—you may be aware that she has suffered from a weak heart for some years.

'I imagine whoever is doing this may be only too well aware of that.'

Jonathan showed him to the left, shook his hand, and Jonathan shook his head.

'This is, thankfully, something I have never come across in thirty years of dealing with trust funds. I wish you the very best of luck in getting to the bottom of it.'

Chapter Four

It was far too early for lunch, but while he was in the big city, Robert decided to exercise his expenses by, first of all, taking a taxi to the Savoy and then treating himself to coffee and extras.

Considering his options, he decided to take a punt on visiting Jasmine Hunt—the elder of the two sisters who happened to live near Portsmouth—on his route home.

He had her number and, after a few moments, a rather quiet, subdued voice came on the phone.

'You won't know me, but I have been asked by your sister, Rose, to come and see you about a private matter. We share suites in the same hotel.'

There was hesitation at the other end.

'It's a while since I was in contact with Rose,' she said. 'Is it something important?'

'Yes, I would say it is. I am in London at the moment and could call on you late this afternoon on my way back to the island.'

Again, there was hesitation, before she replied rather testily, 'Oh, all right,' and ended the call.

No love lost there, Robert concluded.

He arrived in Portsmouth at about four o'clock and took a taxi from the station to Jasmine's address in Southsea.

It was a rather run-down old bungalow in a row of similar properties about three streets back from the sea.

When she opened the door, Robert noted immediately that she appeared much older than Rose, although he had been assured that she was about ten years younger.

He was invited into a living room smelling faintly of lavender and guided to a small padded chair.

'Can I offer you tea, Mr-?'

'Granger. Yes, that would be very nice.'

She shuffled away and was gone for about ten minutes, during which he could hear the rattle of cups.

An old father clock ticked steadily away in the hall.

She returned with a tray and sat down slowly.

'I'm a widow and live alone—but I suppose Rose told you that. You did not tell me on the phone the purpose of your visit.'

Robert took a sip of tea which was not half bad.

'I'll come right to the point. Your sister has been receiving some very unpleasant threatening letters.

'You know she has a bad heart and it has affected her badly. It seems that someone would like to see her dead—I put it as bluntly as that.'

Jasmine seemed genuinely shocked and spilt a little of her tea.

'Whoever would do such a thing?'

'Well, you have to ask who would benefit from her death. That is the only feasible motive. The only obvious persons are her nephews and nieces who inherit.'

Jasmine started to tremble.

'You surely don't think any of my three boys would do such a thing?'

Robert stood up and paced about the room.

'However unlikely—we cannot rule it out with so much money at stake.'

'Well, David, my eldest, is happily married with three children. He has a good job and has never mentioned the trust fund.

'Paul is single and lives and works in Holland. He visits about every two months. I know that he thinks the world of his Aunt Rose. He spent many holidays with her as a boy.'

Robert consulted his notes.

'That leaves James. So far as Rose is aware, he was living here with you.'

'He was very unsettled after a long-term relationship broke down—he was here for a while but has moved to Southampton in a flat.'

'Is he working?'

'I think he is unemployed and looking for building work.'

'No doubt he is aware of the trust—like the others?'

'I suppose so. He has never mentioned it.'

'I would like his address.'

Jasmine got unsteadily to her feet and moved to a desk in the corner.

She returned with a small piece of paper with James's address scrawled on it—probably in his handwriting.

'You won't be unkind to him, will you?' she asked suddenly.

It occurred to him that he must seem a rather menacing figure to her, living so quietly alone.

'I just need to ask him a few questions,' Robert replied.

Chapter Five

Robert left Jasmine feeling extremely sorry for her.

There was no evidence in her lifestyle that Rose had spread generosity in her direction.

He wondered just what she would make of a massive inheritance in her present reduced state.

Having ruled out the other two sons, that left James.

Armed with his address, Robert made his way to Southampton and, as it was late, booked himself overnight into a Travelodge.

Refreshed after a good breakfast the next morning, he took a taxi and found himself in a dingy run-down part of the city.

It took him some time to find the flat, up two flights of unlit stairs and along a corridor, all of which had seen better days.

He found the door with its number hanging loose and upside down.

There was no immediate answer to his knock, but eventually, a tousled bleary-eyed middle-aged man, with a loose shirt hanging out over an ample stomach, opened the door a crack.

'Your mother gave me your address,' said Robert, hoping this would elicit some reaction.

'What do you want?'

'I've come to talk to you about your Aunt Rose.'

James wiped a hand across his face and tried to sober up.

'Why—has something happened to her?'

'If you'll let me in, I can tell you.'

James shuffled back a pace or two, leaving Robert to squeeze in.

The living room was a predictable shambles with empty bottles all over the floor and empty food takeaway bags on the one chair visible.

'I suppose you are aware of the trust your grandfather set up—Rose is enjoying the fund at the moment.

'She has been receiving some nasty messages and threats. Do you know anything about that?'

James was now pulling himself together and could recognise an accusation when it was coming his way.

He sneered at Robert and started to become belligerent.

'You accusing me, are you?' he asked.

'I'm not accusing anyone—yet,' said Robert quietly, trying to defuse the situation.

'Well, I don't know nothing about any threats—I ain't seen Rose for years.

'She means nothing to me and I wouldn't want to see her after the way she's treated me mum.'

Robert leaned back against the only table in the room.

'I went to see your mum yesterday. She didn't think you would know anything about the threats but I had to check.'

James sneered again.

'What are you—a fucking detective?'

'Yes, in a way. I'm just trying to find the person who has been sending threatening letters.'

'Why would I want to do that anyway?'

Robert thought there was no good holding back.

'Because you and the others stand to inherit a lot of money when your aunt dies. Someone is trying to push her over the edge.'

James seemed to see the funny side of this.

'Good luck to them.'

Robert decided that there was nothing to be gained by prolonging their discussion.

He excused himself and left hurriedly.

This was one suspect he could definitely rule out.

Chapter Six

Robert felt that the net was very slowly tightening as he made his way to the home of Ellen Carstairs, the younger of the two sisters.

Her address in Gloucester appeared to be, from what he remembered of the city, in a rather more salubrious area than Jasmine's very humble home.

He took a train and taxi, deciding that, as with James, it was probably more likely to be productive if he did not signal his presence in advance.

The smart four-bedroomed house stood in its own grounds.

Someone with skill had been at work in the small but very smart front garden.

Before he had reached the front door, it opened and a small, bespectacled woman in her seventies came out to greet him.

'I was rather expecting you,' she said. 'Jasmine told me you are on the trail of someone who has been threatening Rose.

'It certainly isn't me—and I think I can vouch for Craig and Harriet—but you had better come in.'

The house was warm and welcoming.

'I can't forgive Daddy for overlooking Jasmine and me but, thanks to my late husband, I am doing all right.

'Sit down and I will make us some tea.'

She disappeared and Robert settled into a very comfortable settee.

He was feeling distinctly weary.

Ellen returned with a smart tray and even smarter tea cups and saucers, flanked by a silver teapot of the kind rarely spotted today.

It was all rather last century.

'Wel,l I'm sorry for Rose—I know she hasn't been well for some time and this is dreadful behaviour by someone.

'I know you think it's one of the children who are to inherit but I can't recall Craig or Harriet referring to their future inheritance since it was first mentioned years ago.

'Craig has moved to Scotland and works on the rigs. I don't see him often.

'Harriet has a small farm in rural Wales—lots of sheep and she struggles to get by but she loves the life and wouldn't do anything else.'

'Is she married?'

'Not at the moment. She met someone a few months ago—a whirlwind romance. She's getting married in a couple of weeks.'

'You must be very excited for her.'

'Yes, I am. She's not had a serious relationship before. I don't know much about him but she brought him here once and he seemed very nice.'

'What does he do for a living?'

'I think he's in sales—works away a lot.'

They chatted amiably for an hour or so, but Robert could feel his eyes drooping and excused himself.

He checked into a hotel and gave himself a hot shower before collapsing into bed and crashing out for several hours.

He was woken by his phone.

To his surprise it was Jean-Claude.

'I am sorry to disturb you, Mr Robert, but there has been a crisis—your aunt is very upset and seeing the doctor—you must get back as soon as possible.'

Chapter Seven

In view of the cryptic call from Jean-Claude, Robert dressed immediately, booked out and organised a taxi.

The driver looked surprised but more than delighted to drive him overnight down to Portsmouth, where he could catch the morning hover to the island.

He cursed the fact that he no longer drove.

He had his reasons, which not everyone would understand, but, being retired and fairly wealthy, he could afford to go anywhere on the island by taxi.

He arrived at the hotel at about ten o'clock and went straight to Rose's suite.

Dr Jones, her private GP, was just leaving.

'Ah, Mr Granger, she will be so glad to see you back.

'I've given her a rather large sedative so she may be fairly sleepy and not able to answer all your questions intelligibly for a while. Just bear with her—I'm sure you understand.'

Robert thanked him and slipped quietly into the room.

Rose was not immediately to be seen, and Robert carried on into her spacious bedroom where he found her tucked up in bed, with her eyes closed.

He was just about to tiptoe out, trying not to disturb her, when an eye opened and she called out, 'Robert, is that you?'

He came back and sat on the end of the bed.

She made a determined effort to sit up but then slumped back onto her pillows.

'I've had the most awful experience,' she managed to say.

'You know I go to the hairdressers in Newport once a week. I have a regular taxi with Anton who has been taking me for years.'

Telling the story seemed to revive her and she sat up.

'On the way, we saw a large black car following. At one point, it came alongside with blackened windows and I thought it was trying to drive us off the road.

'Then it drove on very fast. Later, as I was getting out, I saw the car parked nearby. I had almost reached the door of the salon when two tall men dressed in black, with masks covering their faces, came either side of me.

'I was terrified. Then one said quietly, 'It's time to die'—nothing else.

'They walked away and I went into the salon almost ready to collapse. People nearby came to help but the men had gone.

'Anton had stayed in the taxi and did not see any of it.

'I was really shaken and having my hair done helped to calm me down.

'When I got back, I found one of those envelopes had been delivered by hand—nobody saw who it was—and it simply read in capital letters: 'IT'S TIME TO DIE'.

'I can't take this any more.'

Robert reached over and took her hand.

'Whoever is behind this is using some organisation to do their dirty work. Those two men were professionals—out to frighten you but not to go far enough to break the law.

'Still, I think the point is well past when the police should be involved.'

Rose shook her head.

'No, I don't want to advertise this to the world—you know what the police would do—I would have the press on my back in a flash.'

'Yes, you're right. We'll have to intercept the next messenger—they must think they have you on the run and there are bound to be further letters.

'I'll have a word with Jean-Claude and we'll work out some scheme to trap whoever delivers the next letter.'

Chapter Eight

Robert went to have a conference with Jean-Claude.

He was very shocked and upset.

'I never thought it would be necessary to have a camera installed to see who entered and left the hotel, but I will install it now.

'I have made enquiries and a local firm will come tomorrow.

'At least then we will see when the next envelope is delivered.'

Robert thanked him for this and added that he would be keeping a watch on the camera day and night.

Over the next day or two, Rose seemed to have recovered, and was eating and sleeping normally.

The doctor paid a second visit and pronounced himself satisfied.

All was quiet for three days and nights.

Robert had forced himself to stay awake. The camera gave a sweeping view of the hotel entrance and the drive for a distance of perhaps forty metres. It was about two a.m.

Suddenly, he spotted a large black car driving very slowly towards the hotel.

He left his room and descended to the ground floor.

The hotel entrance was lit and he crept forward, keeping out of sight.

A figure emerged from the car and came forward quite casually towards the entrance.

It was clearly a man—about six feet tall—dressed in black and wearing a mask.

The door had been left unlocked and slightly open.

As the man bent to place something into the letterbox, Robert wrenched open the door and pulled the unsuspecting man inside, landing a sharp kick to his vitals.

The man doubled up in pain. Robert followed with a heavy blow to the stomach and a punch to the jaw.

The man was barely conscious as Robert pulled off the mask, at the same time slamming the door shut and locking it.

Now, whoever was still in the car could not get in to assist.

Robert grabbed the man and forced him into the hotel lobby.

There, the lights went on and Jean-Claude appeared, brandishing a large kitchen knife.

Robert forced the man down into a chair and stood over him.

'There's no need for this, mate—we're only delivering a letter,' the man pleaded.

Robert slapped him hard across the face.

'Tell us who sent you.'

The man started to wipe blood from his face.

'Honest, mate—we never met him. This is strictly a contract job. We only have a phone contact.'

Robert looked at Jean-Claude, who was shaking his head.

'Doesn't even have the guts to do his own dirty work'.

He spat in disgust.

Robert now played his trump card.

'How much are you—and your mate—being paid for this?'

'Five grand—up to now.'

'Suppose we top that up to seven—and you let your contact know that you've been cobbled and had a better offer to give up.'

'That will make him mad.'

Robert smiled.

'That's the idea. It may flush him out—assuming it's a 'he', of course.'

The man thought about it for a moment.

'Payment guaranteed? After all, we're in business, mate. It's all the same to us.'

'Payment guaranteed—providing you ring now and tell him exactly what I told you to say.'

The man took out his phone, shrugged rather apologetically, and made the call.

'I left a message – but I think it was quite clear'.

Chapter Nine

Robert knew that his investigation was now nearing its end.

The one remaining niece was Harriet Carstairs, living her lonely existence on a remote Welsh farm.

This was in deepest Powys and he carefully plotted a journey that would take him as near as possible by train and, finally, taxi.

When he tackled Rose about the payoff to the two hired 'assassins', she pooh-poohed it as a mere trifle—of no more account in the scheme of things than his many expensive train and taxi journeys.

It was a means to an end and that was all that mattered.

Again, he decided not to warn Harriet in advance—figuring that it was highly unlikely that he would not find a small sheep farmer at home.

The taxi wound its way along a narrow rutted track which he had been confidently assured by a passing shepherd would lead him to his destination.

Eventually, he spotted a trail of smoke rising upwards from a stone cottage, which he assumed to be the farmhouse—or its equivalent in these parts.

As a precaution, not wishing to be stranded there, he asked the taxi driver to wait, assuring him that his visit would be short.

He alighted and started to pick his way along the path leading to the cottage when he was greeted by a very aggressive sheepdog.

As the dog approached looking to take no prisoners, a woman, Robert took to be Harriet, appeared, calling loudly to the dog which immediately backed off and sat obediently at Robert's feet.

'Don't you worry about Jack,' said Harriet as she hurried to welcome him.

'I was expecting you—Mum told me all about Aunt Rose and the trouble she has been having. You are very welcome but I don't think I can help you in any way.'

She suddenly gave a loud guffaw.

'It certainly isn't me playing silly games, I can assure you.'

She beckoned Robert into the farm cottage where he found himself in a surprisingly large kitchen.

He was led to a huge farm chair and he could smell that she had been baking—that lovely bready smell which took him back to his childhood.

'I've visited everybody else so I felt I must make the effort,' said Robert.

'It's a long way to come—and not the easiest journey.'

'You can say that again—but I envy you living in such a beautiful part of the country. Don't you get lonely sometimes?'

He hoped to encourage her to mention her fiancé and impending nuptials.

'My life has turned around since I met Huw,' she said.

'Did my mum tell you that I'm getting married next month?'

'Yes, congratulations. I hope you will be very happy. Is Huw not about? I would have liked to meet him.'

'Not at the moment—he works away a lot.'

Robert noticed a photograph prominently displayed on the sideboard—showing Harriet and a tall dark-haired man, presumably Huw, in a fond embrace.

'I have to tell you that events have moved on in the last few days.

It seems that someone was paying an organisation to cause all the trouble. We don't know yet who is behind it but we have paid off the men carrying out the threats and the culprit now knows he or she is on their own.'

Harriet seemed impressed.

'So do you know who is behind it?'

'Not yet but the net is closing. Your aunt has been very ill but is picking up now. She feels that there won't be any more threats. She is very relieved.'

'I told Huw all about it. He will be very pleased it's all over.'

Chapter Ten

Robert returned to the island to review the situation.

By now Jean-Claude had become so involved that Rose was only too happy for him to be brought into their discussions.

They sat down in Rose's suite and Robert recounted his visits and discussions.

He had already ruled out the two aunts as in any way suspicious—he could not imagine them using such an outside agency.

Reviewing David and Paul—their circumstances, as described by their mother, effectively ruled them out.

Then there was James, the down-and-out son living in squalor.

He seemed—apart from any other consideration— to have little or no clue about his impending inheritance.

In fact, there seemed to be little knowledge or interest by anyone he had seen about their future prospects, which was surprising had they known its true extent.

That begged the question as to just how much Jonathan Scott had disclosed to all or any of them.

That left Craig and Harriet in the frame.

Craig was hardly likely to be involved working away on the rigs.

Robert's focus was now on Harriet. She would know about the trust and just how much of this had she passed on to the mysterious Huw.A man who had come unexpectedly into her spinsterish life, swept off her feet and was now about to marry her.

The timing of all this led to the gravest suspicions that this Huw was, in reality, a man who suddenly found that he was about to marry a gold mine.

A man in a hurry who, Robert guessed, would not be above using a shady organisation to carry out his dirty work—a man in a hurry not prepared for nature to take its course.

Now that he knew his agents had been bought off, he was on his own and Robert guessed that he might be desperate.

Desperate enough to pay a visit to the hotel in person.

Having paid out a sizable sum for nothing—as he would assume from Harriet that Rose was now recovering from her ordeal and assumed herself in the clear—he would no doubt feel that he must put her under pressure again as soon as possible.

This meant that Robert and Jean-Claude must renew their vigil urgently.

Assuming that Huw had never actually visited the locale, he would not be prepared for the camera positioned to trap anyone approaching, day or night.

They decided to take turns keeping watch.

A couple of days and nights went by without any suspicious activity.

Then, on the third night, while Robert was on the watch, he heard what he thought was a vehicle approaching.

There was no sign of it on camera—he assumed that the driver had parked some way from the hotel entrance.

Then, the shadow of a man could be seen stealthily approaching.

Robert slipped downstairs and hid near the entrance.

The man now approached the door and, as he leant forward to place something in the letterbox, Robert flung the door back and grabbed the man, pulling him into the entrance.

This time he was not as lucky as before.

The man slipped out of his grasp and managed to land a heavy blow to Robert's jaw.

He was now away into the lobby and Robert recovered quickly and chased him up the staircase onto the first floor.

He could see the man trying the door into his own suite, and entering it.

The room was in darkness as Robert followed—the only light came from beyond his balcony.

The man had seen this and made for it as the obvious means of escape.

He had just reached it and was on the point of climbing over when Robert caught him and tried to drag him back.

They struggled and Robert thought he had succeeded in hauling him in, but the grip on the man's coat proved illusory.

A moment later, the man lost his balance, gave a despairing cry and toppled back.

The fall was about fifteen feet and the landing was not pretty.

By this time, Jean-Claude had joined him to gaze at the figure sprawled on the terrace below.

They raced downstairs to see the damage.

The man had landed on his back, and there was blood seeping from his head.

Even in this half-light Robert could see that the man could be readily identified from the cosy picture on Harriet's wall. It was Huw.

Jean-Claude left to call an ambulance and the police.

They decided, in view of the hour, not to disturb Rose who had slept peacefully throughout this mayhem in the next suite.

The following morning, they regaled her with the night's events.

'Now it really is all over.'

Paradise Betrayed

Chapter One

'Jean-Claude – did you know I had a sister?'

He was bringing Robert a plateful of the most delightful cooked breakfast.

'That is indeed 'une surprise, mon ami',' replied Jean-Claude.

'When I say a sister—that is not strictly 'vrai'—in fact, she is a half-sister—we had different fathers.'

They had a habit of lapsing into odd bits of French from time to time.

Robert felt that, bearing in mind his rather isolated existence, Jean-Claude had become a true friend, as well as the proprietor of this very special little hotel.

'I assume—'mon ami', that she has been in touch. Will you be inviting her to visit you here?'

'This very day—she will be joining me for tea—no doubt you will be offering us some of your special patisseries.'

'Sans doute,' said Jean-Claude, and departed to allow Robert to tuck into his feast.

As he had not seen Patricia for some fifteen years, he had no idea how she had fared over the interim.

Rumour had it that she had paired up with and then, rather violently, separated from her partner, but the details had never trickled through to Robert.

She would now be forty-five or so—he was not exactly sure.

So far as he knew, she had been involved in journalism—every now and then he would come across an article of a somewhat vitriolic nature penned by her.

She had been part of the London 'scene'—a trendy lot of which Robert had never been particularly enamoured.

After such an interval—although they exchanged obligatory birthday and Christmas greetings—it was a mystery to Robert why she should suddenly be descending on him.

Her email had been quite curt—for a somewhat extravagant wordsmith, she could be extremely abrupt.

'Coming to see you!! Expect me at 3.'

No enquiry whether the visit would be convenient—even whether he would actually be around.

Just an assumption that he would be there at her convenience in time for afternoon tea.

As it happened, he had planned to do some shopping in Newport, but it was more to pass the time than anything and could wait.

He felt time hanging rather heavy and spent some time running along the beach following his usual fitness regime.

Even after retirement he felt obliged to keep himself in trim, if only to preserve his self-respect.

It was a long shot now, but he ever lived in expectation that something special might be required of him.

It was barely half-past-two when he heard a car draw up, and looked down from the front window of his suite, to see a fashionably dressed blonde woman emerging from a parked taxi.

This he assumed to be his sister, and he hurried down to meet her as she was paying for her fare.

As he approached, she turned, gave a brief smile and said, 'Would you mind giving him a tip, sweetie—I'm completely out of change.'

'Where did he pick you up?' asked Robert.

'From the ferry—the one from Lymington.'

'Then he's brought you quite a way.'

Robert reached into his pocket and found a ten-pound note—that he felt was the least the taxi driver could expect, but he seemed content enough.

'Let me look at you,' she gushed, turning him round to inspect him thoroughly like a prized horse.

'You've certainly aged pretty well—how long is it—fifteen years?'

'About. You look pretty good yourself—for all your extravagant lifestyle.'

She aimed a mock punch at him.

'You're still a tease—are you going to invite me in?'

She grabbed his arm and he led her into the lobby and up to his suite—where she settled herself immediately into the most comfortable chair.

He could wait no longer.

'To what do I owe the honour of this visit?'

Patricia let out a long sigh.

'Settle back—it's a long story.'

Chapter Two

At this point, Jean-Claude arrived with an elegant tray of tea and a plate of enticing patisseries.

Patricia was immediately impressed and lost no time tucking into a choice example.

She poured herself a cup of tea and sank back into her chair.

'I have to tell you straight away that I am on the rum. I am being stalked by my former partner, Gerry Finch. We broke up about a month ago—at least, I broke it off against his will. We were together off and on for five years.

'He's a wheeler-dealer—into all sorts.

'He went to prison briefly for dealing coke.

'He's got the charm of the devil. We'd be apart and I'd swear that was it, but somehow he always managed to persuade me back.

'I've been in publishing for a while and you might know that I wrote a couple of books—chick-lit stuff but they sold well and one of them was optioned for a film.

'With the spoils, Gerry persuaded me to invest in some valuable jewellery—all bought with my money, of course, but he's now claiming a half share as he's on his uppers.'

'Where do you store it?' asked Robert.

Patricia laughed heartily.

'It's all on me-' and she proudly displayed rings on her fingers of each hand, a series of bracelets on both wrists and three or four necklaces of various lengths.

'I suppose that's one way of protecting your assets,' Robert replied with a smile.

'There's nothing cheap, I can assure you. The resale value is, of course, miles less than I paid up front but we are talking about a hundred thousand at least.'

'Then, the sooner you can store it in a secure place the better. The hotel has a small safe downstairs which will do for the time being.

'Longer term, it should really be in a bank. Where do you bank?

'In London—and I don't plan to return there for the time being. I can work from home anywhere at the moment.'

Robert went to the window where he had a clear view of the drive leading to the hotel entrance.

There was nothing in sight.

'When did you last see Gerry?'

Patricia grimaced.

'This afternoon as I was leaving the boat. He saw me and started to chase but I hailed a taxi and beat him to it.

'Now he knows I'm on the island and don't live here but he will soon figure that I'll have to find somewhere to stay. Luckily, he doesn't know about you.

'If he finds me he'll be upset. He had a go at me a couple of times while we were together.'

Robert was thinking hard.

'There's a put-u-up in my bedroom which I can set up in here for the time being.

'I suggest, in the meantime, you go into the bathroom and divest yourself of all the jewellery so we can put it in the safe.'

She departed and Robert rang down to Jean-Claude.

'My guest has some valuables which she needs to put in the safe.

'Is there anything being stored in there at the moment?'

'Rien,' replied Jean-Claude. 'I will meet you and give you a key—normally I reserve it strictly for myself.'

'Much appreciated.'

The jewellery was secreted in a large bag and placed in the safe.

Robert retained the key.

Chapter Three

It was a real pleasure catching up after so many years.

Their mother had been a bit of a goer in her early days, on the circuit and living it up with Robert's father, a banker whose affluent circle ensured a giddy round of enjoyments.

After his premature death, his mother had played the field for a few years, before latching on to a rather elderly lawyer. Perhaps Patricia was unexpected, certainly rather an encumbrance.

If she had calmed down after that it was not immediately apparent to those of her inner circle, before her second husband faded away quietly.

By the time Patricia was in her teens, Robert had long since fled the coop.

He was in the army before starting his detective agency, a far cry from her world, and their paths never crossed.

Robert supposed that they both had a bit of the maverick in their natures, inherited from their mother.

They chewed the fat until a late hour, having had the luxury of a late dinner delivered to the suite with a real flourish by Jean-Claude.

Robert brought the put-u-up into the living room and retired to give Patricia as much privacy as he could.

The following morning, he was awake at six as usual and tip-toed in to find her curled up fast asleep.

He disappeared to his morning run before breakfast, contemplating how he could contrive to prevent Patricia from being traced by the vengeful Gerry.

The island is not, of course, large, but it was sod's law that they would come across one another the longer she stayed with him, as he would be bound to take her out and about.

Later in the morning, Patricia decided that she had seen enough o the hotel and would like to visit Newport to do some shopping.

As Robert no longer drove, this would mean hiring a taxi on his usual way.

Patricia was surprised and impressed that he travelled everywhere in such a lordly fashion.

They swept into Newport and were deposited in the town centre.

For a few minutes, they simply did a spot of window shopping.

Robert was not paying attention or he would have spotted a man in a raincoat sporting dark glasses, who was following them at a discreet distance.

A while later in a busy street, Patricia was walking ahead of Robert as he stopped to look in the window of a sports store.

Suddenly, a car drew into the curb, stopped and a man leapt out of, what Robert took to be, the passenger seat—in fact, it was a left-hand-drive vehicle.

He grabbed Patricia and forced her across the front seat, leaping back in and setting off without regard to the traffic; horns sounding furiously at him.

As luck would have it, his progress was impeded by a queue of traffic which had conveniently stopped up ahead, giving Robert time to hail a passing taxi.

He ordered the driver to keep the offending car in front in sight.

With a quick twenty quid shoved in his pocket, the taxi driver had no difficulty with this and, although the car in front raced away at the first opportunity, they were able to follow close enough to keep it in sight.

After a mile or two, the first swerved violently and turned into a trading estate.

For a few moments, it was lost to sight but then appeared ahead, stationary.

Robert ordered his driver to pull up about fifty metres behind.

He jumped out, as the front door of the car ahead suddenly swung open, and Patricia was flung out onto the road in a heap.

The car then drove off, with the door swinging wildly until it was out of sight.

Robert raced up to help Patricia to her feet.

She was angry, upset and shaking.

'He's been following me since I landed—he knows where I'm staying and he knows about the jewels.'

'A friend of Gerry's—did you recognise him?' asked Robert.

'He's no friend of Gerry but he must have heard about the jewels somehow.

'He threatened me—meet him outside the town hall tomorrow at ten with the jewels or he will come after me.

'And he was pretty explicit about what he would do to me then-'

Chapter Four

Robert held Patricia for a minute to ensure that she was in one piece.

The taxi was still waiting patiently for them down the road.

They walked slowly together, Robert holding her close for comfort.

'Never seen anything like that' the taxi driver commented, shaking his head.

'A good thing you were there to help her, mate.'

They climbed into the back together, Robert holding her hand.

The rest of the journey was spent in silence.

When they reached the hotel, Robert led Patricia up to his suite and rang Jean-Claude.

'There's been a bit of trouble in town,' he said. 'Patricia is rather shaken up. Could you bring us one of your large cafetieres—and a couple of double brandies?'

'Mon dieu,' replied Jean-Claude, 'It sounds serious.'

Patricia went off to clean up and inspect her bruises from being thrown to the ground.

Luckily, nothing was broken, but her clothing had taken most of the impact.

Jean-Claude arrived looking very concerned, decided that discretion was the best part of valour, and swiftly left them to it.

After a long cup of strong coffee and knocking back the brandies, Patricia had pulled herself together enough to talk rationally again.

'I think it's time to review the situation,' said Robert.

'We don't have much time in view of the threats you received and the demands made. Tell me more about this man. You say that you had never seen him before?'

Patricia was thinking hard.

'At the back of my mind, I seem to remember seeing him drinking with Gerry in a pub once, but I can't recall exactly when or where.'

'Can you describe him? I know it all happened very fast and you were in shock.'

'He had a moustache and short beard—oh, and a fairly livid scar on his right cheek.'

'That should make him easy to identify.'

Robert finished his coffee and left the brandy for later.

He realised that he had some hard thinking to do and some tough decisions to make.

'To my mind, there are three things we have to decide—and none of them easy.

'First, this man who threatened you is obviously dangerous and we can't underestimate what he might do.

'You are very vulnerable while on the island. He could be anywhere and I kick myself for not staying close to you this morning.

'Let us start by assuming that there is no way you are going to meet him tomorrow and hand over the jewellery.'

'You are darned right. Over my dead body.'

Robert smiled.

'We certainly don't want it to come to that!'

'Then what is your plan?'

'I'm afraid I now have to ask you a difficult question but a lot could turn on your answer.

'I know that Gerry is not flavour of the month just now but he's clearly crazy about you, otherwise, he would not be pursuing you up and down dale.

'Be honest—you have spent years together on and off, but there's something that always pulls you back together.

'Do you really love him?'

Patricia sighed.

'If I'm honest—there is never likely to be anyone else for me.'

Chapter Five

Robert was gratified that at least the first part of his plan could now take shape.

He leant across and took Patricia's hand.

'Bearing in mind what you have just admitted, I am going to make a suggestion that you may not like.'

'Go ahead.'

'In the present situation, it makes no sense to go on fighting Gerry over the jewellery.

'I accept that you feel that you paid for it—but most of the time, Gerry was living with you—and you can see why he feels he is entitled to his fair share.

'I am going to suggest that you give up the fight over that—and that we can ask Gerry for something in return.'

'Let's say then that I accept his entitlement—what can he offer?'

'At the moment, the most urgent problem is how to get the man off your back without parting with the jewels. Gerry is somewhere on the island at the moment looking for you.

'Can you contact him on your phone and arrange to meet?'

Patricia was obviously surprised at this suggestion.

'I can still get hold of him. Are you sure that's a good idea?'

Robert stood up and paced around.

'It's the only way to resolve this whole mess.'

Patricia got out her phone and was quite gratified to find Gerry on the other end.

'Hello, sweetheart. Where are you?'

Patricia looked at Robert for guidance.

'Tell him we'll meet him at the King's Arms in town in about an hour.'

Patricia passed on the message and explained that she was staying with her brother who would be coming to meet him.

'That detective fellow?'

'Robert—he's looking after me. I want him along when we meet.'

'Whatever you say, sweetheart. I'll find the pub. See you later.'

Robert ordered a taxi and they sat down to plan their strategy.

'You'll tell him what happened to me?'

'I'll lay it on thick.'

The taxi arrived and they sat quietly watching the scenery go by.

They were dropped close to the King's Arms.

On entering the bar, Patricia saw that Gerry had already arrived and was downing a large whisky and soda.

He jumped up with a delighted look on his face.

To his surprise, he shook Robert's hand enthusiastically.

'I'm grateful you brought her to me—I was getting tired of chasing after her.'

They settled at a table and Gerry went to order them both a drink.

'You had better do the talking,' said Patricia quietly.

Gerry returned with the drinks, sat down and was gazing at Patricia.

'Are you all right, sweetheart? You don't look quite yourself.'

This gave Robert the intro.

'It's not surprising,' he said, 'She's had a nasty shock. Somebody has been shadowing your every move.

'We were in town, when a man pulled up and bundled her into a car. I managed to chase after him.

'After a while, he threw her out onto the road and drove off.

'He obviously knows about the jewellery you and Patricia have bought—and that it is highly valuable.

'That is what he is after. He told her to be outside the town hall at ten tomorrow with the jewels.

'He made some dire threats if she fails to turn up.'

All the while Robert could see that Gerry was getting more and more furious.

'Can you describe this character?' he asked.

'He had a short beard and tash—with a scar on his right cheek.'

Gerry thumped the table, wobbling the drinks.

'It's that sod, Roddy Kemp. I'll bloody kill him!'

Chapter Six

Gerry took a sip of his whisky and sat back.

'I met the bloke in prison—we shared a cell for a week or two. By that time, Pat and I had bought some of the gems.

'When I got out, Roddy and I had a couple of drinks together—I never really cottoned the bloke—but perhaps I said more than I ought to have done.

'He's a cunning thief and must have decided to keep an eye on me. He's also managed to hook into my messages somehow.'

Robert now saw the chance to put forward his plan.

'Speaking of the jewels—Patricia has decided to do a deal with you—she will share the proceeds down the middle—in return for your sorting out this Roddy once and for all.'

Gerry stood up and once again offered Robert his hand.

'It's a deal.'

'I suggest we meet up outside the town hall at about nine in the morning. Roddy is unlikely to be there until nearer ten.'

'Agreed.'

It was obvious that Gerry was parting with Patricia very reluctantly and, as they left the pub, he stood watching them walk away.

Time hung heavy for the rest of the day.

The following morning dawned sunny and bright.

Jean-Claude brought them both breakfast at Robert's suite.

Patricia was a bag of nerves and hardly ate.

By contrast, Robert ate a hearty meal.

At just after twenty to nine, a taxi arrived and they travelled in silence into town.

On the steps of the town hall they found Gerry already waiting.

'We'll keep out of sight until Roddy arrives, then we confront him.'

'That's one way of putting it,' said Gerry menacingly.

They kept watch as the town gradually came to life.

'Let's just hope nobody much is around when he comes,' said Gerry.

At around five minutes to ten, they saw a figure approaching.

Roddy was looking around him furtively, but there was nobody in the vicinity.

He took up a position where he could observe Patricia approaching.

Ten o'clock came and went, and they could see from their vantage point that he was becoming nervous and agitated.

This was the moment when Robert urged Patricia forward.

As she approached, he turned towards her and, in that instant, Gerry stepped out from behind him.

'Hello, Rod—fancy meeting you here,' said Gerry in mock greeting.

He grabbed Roddy by the shoulders and short-armed him out of sight.

It required little imagination to appreciate what was taking place.

Shouting, loud voices, then unmistakable thumps and the sound of a body slumping to the ground as Roddy got what was coming to him.

It all seemed reminiscent to Robert of earlier days.

'I hope you didn't hurt him too much,' Robert remarked, as Gerry emerged with a smile on his face.

Patricia had watched the whole episode in fear and trembling.

Gerry walked over and took her in his arms.

'You don't have to worry about him anymore,' he reassured her.

The three of them walked off together.

'Time for a stiff drink,' said Robert.

'The drinks are on me.'

Paradise Proposed

Chapter One

'It feels so quiet without Gerry and Patricia,' Robert remarked, as Jean-Claude came in with his breakfast.

He was on his own in the dining room.

Rose Staples, as usual, was taking her meals in her suite upstairs and rarely appeared, save for an occasional descent for afternoon tea with a friend.

These were always like state occasions.

Jean-Clause would take the opportunity of showing off his expertise with exquisite delicacies.

The two remaining residents would be down to breakfast an hour later than Robert, who liked to maintain a certain discipline in his habits.

Paul Cain was a retired accountant suffering from a weak heart.

He spent a great deal of time taking tablets and fussing over health issues, which he was only too willing to indulge if given the opportunity.

Richard Crane was reputed to have friends in high places—now in his eighties, he had become rather lame and rarely took any exercise.

Both of them were now at the mercy of Jean-Claude's excellent cooking.

Robert found them both rather depressing company, particularly in view of the disparity in their ages and fitness.

They would watch rather listlessly from the dining room window as Robert set off in his running gear for the beach.

On this morning, a sharp wind had got up and clouds were scurrying across the sky.

It was late autumn and he was wondering what to do with himself in the run-up to Christmas.

It was rather too cold to contemplate a swim in the sea.

He was turning to go up to his suite when his mobile phone rang.

This was unusual and he was intrigued.

There was a female voice on the other end—not too clear.

'Robert—is that you? It's Diana.'

For a moment, he was totally mystified.

'I'm sorry—do you have the right number?'

'This is the number you gave me when you left—it's Diana. Don't you recognise my voice?'

It suddenly dawned on him.

Diana—his former partner from twenty years ago.

'What a surprise to hear from you—where are you ringing from?'

'I'm at the Premier Inn at Newport. I pushed the boat out and stayed overnight. I need to see you.

'I know you are on the island but I have no idea where you are.'

'I'm living in a hotel on the south of the island. You sit tight and I'll come and get you. Wait in the foyer—I will be as quick as I can.'

A myriad of thoughts and memories passed through Robert's mind as he rang for his usual taxi, which arrived within minutes and whisked him away.

He wondered what on earth could have impelled Diana to contact him after all this time—he surmised that she must be in some kind of trouble.

He had left her with his mobile phone number but they had not been in touch for about twenty years.

Their final parting had been far from a happy one—full of recriminations.

The taxi drew up at the Premier Inn and he saw a woman standing outside the entrance.

Twenty years was a long time and appearances could change radically but, there she was, blonde hair swept back and as striking as ever.

For the first time in ages, he felt a lurch inside.

Chapter Two

He leapt out of the taxi, rushed across and held her in a close embrace.

Emotions long forgotten surged through him. He couldn't stop himself.

She drew back to look at him.

'Well, you've weathered better than I have.'

He denied it, of course.

'Have you settled up at the Premier?' he asked.

She reached into a pocket and produced the bill.

'I'll pay you back later—when we get to my hotel'.

She seemed surprised.

'It sounds very grand.'

'Not really—but it's comfortable and it's home.'

All the time, the reason for her visit was hanging in the air.

He guided her into the back seat of the taxi and he nodded to his driver.

He sat holding her hand unable to resist it. She did not mind.

'So, what has brought you to my door?'

She paused, trying to find the right words.

'It goes back to our last night—that awful day when you walked out and I was glad to see you go.

'Do you remember the weekend before—when we went away to have one last try—it must have happened then.'

Robert was completely in the dark.

'It was only a week or two after you left that I found I was pregnant. I didn't know what to do.

'Things had been so bad between us and you were so wound up in your detective bureau—desperate for work.

'I didn't think I could break it to you then—and, as time went by, I lost my nerve completely.

'I moved away and took a flat in Reading where I had some friends.

'I considered a termination but began to look quite forward to becoming a mother.

'When Gary was born, he looked so like you—our time together wasn't all bad.

'I managed to get a job where I was able to take the baby—time went by and I had no idea what you were doing.

'Gary grew up so fast—he was into school and then a senior.

'We had a few arguments in his teens—he was so like you at times.

'He left school and took a job in a local factory. I thought he was at least content but I was wrong.

'One day, he simply announced he was leaving and going north.

'He had a friend who ran the local stores in a village up in Yorkshire—for a while, he kept in touch then, a month or two ago, he stopped ringing me.

'I got rather frantic. I couldn't get any sense out of anybody and I think they were deliberately trying to fob me off.

'This is a last resort—I didn't know exactly where you were, but I read a report somewhere of one of your cases which mentioned that you live on the Isle of Wight.

'So, I came over to look for you.'

Robert had simply let her tell the story—so much had happened, of which he was totally unaware.

'So, you want me to find him—for both our sakes,' said Robert.

'What you didn't know is that I have been retired for a few years. I live here in a hotel—very happily.

'I think you will like it. You must stay for a while—as my guest.'

Diana suddenly burst into floods of tears.

'You were always such a good detective. I know you'll find him.'

Chapter Three

As they pulled in at the hotel, Robert was surprised to see Jean-Claude there to greet them on the front porch.

He could obviously not wait to see Diana.

'Welcome, madame,' he said, coming forward to shake her hand. 'I trust you will find everything here to your satisfaction.'

She looked up, impressed with the façade and such a welcome.

Robert guided her inside and Jean-Claude carried her suitcase.

'I think we will go up to my suite—could you bring us a cafetiere of your best coffee?'

Jean-Claude nodded and departed.

Once inside, Diana gazed at her surroundings in astonishment.

'This is palatial—and what a view!'

Robert invited her to sit and decided to fill her in with the details of his recent history.

'As you can see, I have rather fallen on my feet. It's a long story but I'm settled here for good—retired and very comfortable.

'I can't deny that I've missed you—and gone over the way we parted hundreds of times, wishing it could all have been different.

'You won't believe the number of times I was on the point of contacting you—but I was afraid of being rebuffed.

'I couldn't face that prospect.'

'It was the same for me,' Diana replied. 'Sheer cowardice in the end.'

Jean-Claude now appeared with the coffee and some of his special cakes.

'We have several rooms vacant at the moment,' he suggested, 'If madame is intending to stay?'

'You are welcome to stay as long as you like—as my guest, of course,' said Robert.

Diana was clearly rather overwhelmed by all this generosity.

Jean-Claude departed, indicating that they had only to let him know their intentions.

'Now, tell me what you know about Gary's movements,' said Robert. 'Once I have a starting point, I can try to pick up his trail.'

'The last I heard from him, he was assisting Peter's father in their village shop. I made a note of it— somewhere in north Yorkshire.'

She reached into her handbag and produced a piece of paper with writing scrawled on it.

'Here it is—Masham. I looked it up on the map— it's right out in the country.'

'I'll set off first thing in the morning,' said Robert. 'In the meantime, we'll sort out a nice room for you and you must stay until I trace and bring him home.'

Diana was shaking her head.

'That might not be as easy as you think,' she said.

'He has an awful stubborn streak.'

'I suppose he gets it from me,' said Robert.

'I can be very persuasive—I'll just play it by ear.'

They spent the rest of the day sorting out Diana's room, agreeing a rate, and Robert re-imbursing her for her stay at the Premier Inn.

Without exactly spelling it out, it was clear that she was very short of money and anxious about losing her job if she was away too long, having used up her normal holiday allowance.

'I don't have any idea how long I shall be away,' said Robert. 'I'll keep in touch every day and let you know how I'm progressing.

'I keep a suitcase packed for just such an eventuality as this.'

Chapter Four

'I assume you keep a photo of Gary on you?' asked Robert as he prepared to leave.

Diana reached into her handbag and produced a small but very distinctive picture—full face and in good light.

'Good looking, like me,' Robert remarked with a smile.

'I always thought he took after me,' Diana said rather defiantly.

Robert made a call to his regular taxi driver, Bill.

He knew that Bill lived on his own and always seemed to be free to take him everywhere.

'How would you like a couple of days up country on me?' asked Robert.

'Just say the word, guvnor—when do you want to leave?'

'Pack an overnight and call for me in about an hour.'

'Will do.'

Robert went to the kitchen where Jean-Claude was busy preparing lunch.

'I have to go away for a few days—will you look after Diana for me? I don't think she's been feeding herself properly for quite a while.'

'Merde! That's a real shame,' said Jean-Claude.

'You may rest assured I will see she is well fed, mon ami.'

Bill turned up right on time and Robert bade farewell to Diana with some reluctance.

He had started to have all his old feelings back— and hoped she was beginning to feel the same.

'Where to?' asked Bill as they sailed out of the drive.

'We need to cross on the ferry to Lymington—then go north as far as Yorkshire.'

'That's quite a stretch. I'll set the satnav for our destination and hope it doesn't take me too far out of the way. I don't entirely trust it.'

It was a bright and breezy crossing and they had coffee and bacon rolls to fortify them.

Once on the mainland, they made good progress.

Bill was a careful but not slow driver—he had spent years as a chauffeur and was used to much more fancy cars than the present Astra—which was quick enough.

'I reckon this will be about five hours,' he remarked as they made their way out of Hampshire.

Bill hailed from Somerset and had rarely ventured very far north.

Robert, on the other hand, had spent many happy holidays around the northeast coast but was not familiar with the Yorkshire dales.

By early afternoon, they approached Masham and parked up in the square.

'I see the village stores over there,' said Robert. 'I hope I won't be too long.'

He approached the shop and found it quiet, with only two elderly customers.

A young man was attending to them.

Robert waited and then, when he was free, went and picked up a couple of items.

'I wonder if you could help me,' said Robert in an attempt to break the ice.

'I'm looking for a young lad called Gary Foster. I was told that he used to work here.'

This request was met by a puzzled frown.

'He did—some time ago. His mother was asking after him. Who are you?'

Robert decided that there was no point making any bones about it.

'I'm his father. I lost contact with him some time ago. You're right that his mother was looking but she drew a blank. What can you tell me about him?'

The young man called out to an assistant to take over the shop.

'Come with me—I need to tell you something.'

He led the way into a room behind the shop.

'You're right that Gary was here—for a time. We used to be pals and, when he got in touch and sounded desperate, I felt sorry for him.

'There wasn't really a job for him here but I took him on.

'I hadn't realised how mixed up he had become. He'd fallen out big time with his mum and lost his job in Reading where they lived.

'After a couple of weeks, I found there was money missing from the till.

'No guesses as to who was responsible. We had a row and I told him to pack up and leave.

'He asked me one favour—if his mum came looking would I fob her off?

'I agreed—not very happily—but I sort of fudged it when she rang.'

'Have you any idea where he went?' asked Robert.

'I heard he got a job in the agricultural store up the road. I know them well but I didn't let on why I'd let Gary go.'

Chapter Five

Robert was given directions to the agricultural store and they set off up the road.

They were impressed with the size of the store and Robert asked Bill to hang on while he made enquiries.

There was a man moving boxes of produce. Robert followed until he placed the boxes on a stall.

'I'm sorry to bother you but I wonder if you have a young lad working here called Gary Foster?'

The man paused and seemed to be searching his memory.

'A lot of young lads come and go—you wouldn't have a photo on you?'

Robert fished out the photo given to him by Diana.

The man stared at it for a few seconds.

'Hang on—I think it's the lad who caused Derek all that trouble—you can talk to him yourself—he's over there.'

He pointed to a large bespectacled elderly man who was checking a delivery.

Robert approached him with some trepidation.

'I believe you employed a young lad named Gary Foster,' he began.

Immediately the man turned hostile.

'Who are you?'

'I'm trying to trace him—I'm his father.'

He was met with some scorn.

'It's a pity you didn't do a better job bringing him up. He caused nothing but trouble here.'

Robert's heart was beginning to sink.

'I gather he's not here any more.'

'We never like involving the police—it tends to get round and give us a bad name—but I was on the point of it.

We took him on to make deliveries and he told us he had a full licence. I was busy at the time and didn't check.

'Within the first two weeks, he had managed to smash up one of our vans.

'He reckoned it was a pure accident but, a week later, he went out with another of our employees and nearly came to grief.

'My grandson was the passenger—he was as frightened as hell with his driving.

'We took him off deliveries and he was working in the stores.

'It was rumoured he was sleeping rough—and he was seen pilfering food.

'We have a strict rule about that—it's out and no second chances.

'It's funny—he was a likeable lad and, in a way, we felt sorry for him.'

Robert could see the familiar pattern and began to dread where all this might lead.

'Has anybody here any idea where he went?'

'Ah—you could ask my grandson, Eric—he's on the tills today. I think he became quite friendly with Gary—he's only recently out of school and quite impressionable.'

Robert thanked him and made his way round the store to the tills.

'Could I have a word with you—I'm Gary's dad.'

The young lad stared at him in surprise.

'He never told me he had a dad—he lived alone with his mum.'

The older girl took charge and suggested they go off and have a chat.

'I lost touch with him,' said Robert. 'I really want to find him now and bring him home.'

'He was obviously in a lot of trouble, was Gary.

'I really liked him—he was a lot of fun. A bit wild you know—he really screwed up here.'

'Did he keep in touch?'

'About two weeks ago—a message on my phone— he had fallen on his feet—got a job in a big shop in Northallerton—Lewis and Cooper. In the High Street— you can't miss it.'

Chapter Six

By now it was late afternoon, and Robert knew they would be unlikely to reach Northallerton before the shops closed.

They decided to settle for an overnight stay at a Travelodge on the A1.

At this time of year, there was no difficulty in obtaining rooms.

'Time for a decent meal,' said Robert. There was no argument from Bill.

They booked in and went round to the restaurant adjacent to the lodge.

To be quite honest, Robert had largely lost his appetite faced with the tide of bad news.

While they waited to be served a hearty meal, Robert reviewed the story so far with Bill.

'If I had only known at the time, it might have turned out quite differently,' he said.

'But, from what you told me about your relationship with his mother, he might have had a difficult time growing up with two warring parents.

'I know that from experience.'

Bill grimaced at the memory and Robert reached over and gave him a reassuring tap on the shoulder.

After the meal, they decided on an early night, intending to make an early start in the morning.

After a good breakfast—not knowing where their next meal was coming from—Robert rang through to Diana.

She was surprised and rather hurt that he had not phoned before.

'I'm sorry, love, but it's been a long and disappointing trail so far.'

'Have you actually found him yet?'

'He's been moving about all over the place—but we have a good clue to follow this morning.

'I'll ring you later. How has Jean-Claude been looking after you?'

She laughed. 'If I stayed here a month I'd put on two stones.'

Reassured, he rang off and they set off down the A1 towards Northallerton.

He remembered it with great affection. There was so much to like about the town—its bustling atmosphere, Barker's the main store where he recalled enjoying some tremendous meals—and Lewis and Cooper.

This he remembered as an amazing shop—not very wide but amazingly deep inside and boasting all sorts of goodies, not least a very good wine section.

If Gary had indeed managed to obtain a job here then he had truly fallen on his feet.

After coffee at Barker's, Robert left Bill to explore the town and arranged to meet up later.

He entered Lewis and Cooper and headed for the back of the shop.

There were all the wines he remembered.

He spotted a likely manager and asked if he could have a word with him in private.

'I am sorry to bother you but my son told me that he had started working here. I found that rather difficult to believe so I thought I would take the bull by the horns and find out for myself.'

'We would not actually disclose details of staff— but as you are his father I will make an exception.'

'His name?'

'Gary Foster.'

He consulted his phone.

'Do you happen to have a photo on you?'

Robert produced it.

'Ah, yes, I recognise him. A real troublemaker. Was very abusive when we told him there were no vacancies. He was seen off the premises by one of our assistants.'

'Do you recall who that was?'

'Yes, Peter Draper—I suppose there's no harm in your having a word with him.'

A few moments later, a young assistant in overalls arrived.

'Do you recall a young man called Gary Foster? He was being offensive—we asked you to see him off the premises.'

Robert noted that Peter Draper was tall and strongly built.

No one was likely to argue with him or take him on.

He nodded immediately.

'A stroppy character—yes—I had to escort him out. He was grumbling all the way. He said he was off to York where he was sure to find work. No one around here appreciated him.'

Chapter Seven

'It sounds like a wild goose chase' Bill remarked when they met up.

'York is a very big I admit - but we can only try'.

Robert spent the journey turning over the stark narrative of Gary's misdeeds.

He was obviously very disturbed and completely out of control.

It was a miracle that he had not yet fallen foul of the police—but it was clearly only a matter of time.

What hope would he have with a criminal record behind him?

They arrived on the outskirts of York.

As they approached the centre, it became crowded—heavy slow moving traffic and visitors everywhere.

They managed to park with some difficulty.

'You must come and have lunch at Betty's,' said Robert. 'It's one of a chain of fabulous cafés—the food is great and the service impeccable.'

'Lead me to it.'

They managed to get a table after queueing for a while, but it was worth it.

Now fortified, they embarked on the task of trying to find a needle in a haystack.

Robert paused to consider what few facts they knew.

Gary was a young man on the loose. He had no job and it was reasonable to suppose that he had no money.

He had probably hitched a lift down to York.

As he had no money, he would have had to beg or steal—or throw himself on the mercy of a food bank.

He would not have been able to afford anywhere to live—in any event, it was an extremely expensive city.

As they passed a man begging in an alleyway off the street, Robert decided to take a chance.

He crouched down next to the man.

'If I offer you money, are you going to blow it on drink or drugs?'

The man looked up at him with pity.

'What's it to you, mate—some sort of social worker? You're wasting your time.'

He turned away, not interested.

'If I was homeless here in York, where would I doss down at night?'

The man laughed. He had very few teeth.

'It can't be nothing to you. Why do you want to know?'

Robert produced the photo.

'Have you seen him around—begging?'

The man shrugged.

'Don't look the type. Too well dressed.'

'But if he were—homeless, like you—where would he likely doss down?'

The man considered.

'Give us a tenner and I might be able to help.'

Robert produced a ten-pound note. The man grabbed and quickly concealed it.

'They don't like dossers where the tourists can see them. You might look the back of the market.'

That was all Robert wanted to know.

They passed the afternoon window shopping and enjoying tea at Betty's

As darkness fell, they returned to the taxi and snoozed for a few hours.

At about eleven o'clock, Robert slipped out, leaving Bill snoring heavily.

He walked quietly through the streets to the market area.

After a while, he spotted the telltale signs—figures wrapped in blankets here and there, tucked away from the pavement.

He had bought a torch and, at the risk of upsetting these unfortunates—and even causing a violent reaction, he passed through them lighting up their faces as they cowered away.

He had almost given up when he spotted a figure, lying alone, fast asleep.

He shone the torch and knew instantly.

'Who are you? What do you want?'

'I'm your father. I've come to take you home.'

Chapter Eight

'Get away—are you some sort of perv?'

Gary shrank back and tried to hide his face.

'Look at me—look at this.'

Robert produced the small photo and shone his torch so that Gary could see it.

'Where did you get that?'

Gary was still suspicious and hostile.

'Where do you think? Your mother gave it to me. I've been looking for you for days.'

Gary was still very nervous.

'How can you be my dad? My mother never mentioned you.'

'We parted before you were born. I only just knew about you when your mother got in touch with me and asked me to find you.'

'I still don't believe you.'

'Then speak to her yourself.'

Robert rang through on his mobile and, after a few moments, Diana answered.

'I've found him. He wants to speak to you. He doesn't believe who I am.'

Gary took the phone hesitantly.

'Mum, is this man truly my dad?'

'Yes, Gary. He's come to bring you back. I'm with him on the Isle of Wight.'

Gary finally seemed convinced, but still shell-shocked.

'Everything all right?' someone nearby called out, hearing the conversation.

'Yes, no worries,' Gary replied.

He got up and rolled up his dirty blanket.

'Leave that. You won't need it anymore.

'We've got a lot of catching up to do.'.

They reached the taxi to find Bill still fast asleep.

When he woke, he was amazed, and delighted, to see Gary.

'Bill has brought me all the way from home,' said Robert. 'If we drive through the night, we should be able to catch the first boat across to the island in the morning.'

They set off with Robert and Gary together in the back.

Now they had hours to go over the long history of Robert and Diana's time together, their parting, and Diana's discovery of her pregnancy.

'I still don't understand why she never told you about me,' said Gary, obviously hurt.

'I know it's hard to understand. But things were so bad between us at the time we parted.'

'So, now you're retired and living in luxury in a hotel.'

'I had a large slice of luck and came into a lot of money. Enough to set me up for life.

'Except that I have hardly enjoyed a peaceful retirement yet.'

They chatted on as the miles flew by and, as the dawn broke, they reached the outskirts of Lymington.

Gary had never been on a sea crossing and stood on deck for the short journey.

They reached the hotel at about ten o'clock.

Diana rushed out to greet them and clasped her arms around Gary.

'You're all just in time for a late breakfast—Jean-Claude style.'

Chapter Nine

The coda to this story is a happy one.

Diana gave notice and moved in with Robert on a temporary basis.

Gary settled in at the hotel and they made no demands on him for the time being.

Robert considered that he should enrol at a local college and start to acquire some education if he was ever to get some decent employment.

Robert decided to donate enough from his capital to buy Diana a modest two-bedroomed property in the Shanklin area.

She and Gary could live together, at least, until he could afford to move away.

Robert and Diana decided that they were still in love—but were better off living apart to prevent the romance turning sour again.

They would spend time together without recriminations.

It was the best solution all round.

THE END

Paradise is Innocence

Chapter One

It was a fine morning and Robert felt he could not miss the chance of an early bathe, although he suspected the sea would still be chilly.

No one was up and about at his small hotel, although he could hear Jean-Claude busy in the kitchen as he passed.

After a good refreshing swim, there would be nothing better to look forward to than one of Jean-Claude's special fry-ups accompanied by his superb coffee.

Robert's usual practice was to run from the beach into the sea and immerse himself as soon as possible to lessen the shock.

He was soon pulling away with strong strokes, taking him out about fifty yards from the shore.

There, he turned onto his back and gazed at the hotel still visible beyond the bushes.

It seemed in that moment that all was well in the best of all possible worlds.

He headed back towards the shore and dried himself on the large towel he always left there.

On entering the hotel, he decided that he had dried enough to sit out having his breakfast.

It was still too early for any of the other residents to be up and about.

He had settled comfortably to await Jean-Claude arriving to take his order when he sensed that someone was lurking behind him.

He turned and was very surprised to see Peter Compton at his elbow, looking distinctly upset.

Peter was a local lawyer Robert had come across who was good company and they often enjoyed a pint or two in one of the local hostelries.

Robert invited him to sit and waited for an explanation for his appearance.

Peter was dressed for the office and had travelled several miles to see Robert.

'I'm in a heap of trouble,' Peter began. 'I didn't know which way to turn and then it struck me that you might be able to help—but it's a long shot.'

'Of course, I'll do anything within my powers to help an old friend.'

'Wait first unto you hear the grizzly details,' said Peter gloomily.

'Can I at least get you a coffee?' asked Robert.

'No, thanks—I just want to get things off my chest'.

And over the next few minutes, it all poured out.

Chapter Two

3 DAYS EARLIER

Peter Compton arrived at his office at about half past eight.

There were the usual emails to answer and a small pile of post

His regular long-term secretary Pat had written a number of messages.

He had a number of calls to make, some left over from the previous day.

His firm, Preston Downs, had withdrawn from a couple of their branch offices in small towns on the island in favour of brand-new premises in Newport, where every element was under one roof.

This meant, in particular, that he had a spacious room with a good view over the bustling town centre.

Whenever he had a spare moment, he could pause and watch the traffic passing by.

His clientele was diverse after he had been established as a partner of the firm for twenty years.

One area in which he professed some expertise was wealth management.

He oversaw the investments of some prestigious clients, whose confidence in him was very reassuring.

From time to time, the auditors would arrive and settle in for a few days to check the firm's accounts.

This was something that they preferred to do, so that, if discrepancies arose,—heaven forbid—they were on the spot to discuss matters with the senior partner, Jim Preston.

They had settled for a day or two in one of the firm's interview rooms, keeping well out of sight.

It was at about ten-thirty when Peter received a message to call in on Jim at his office on the second floor.

There seemed to be nothing unusual about this, as he and Jim would meet and confer quite routinely throughout the working week.

He knocked, as Jim's door was firmly shut, and waited for the usual gruff invitation to enter.

He found Jim sitting, as usual, at his voluminous desk, clearly pretending to check through some papers and not looking up.

Peter entered the room and came forward.

Jim had not looked up but merely invited him to take a seat facing his desk.

Something was clearly up—Peter detected the vibes immediately.

Finally—after an age—Jim looked up but did not appear to be looking at him directly.

'Peter, I asked you to come up because I've had some rather disturbing news from the auditors.

'Do you recall that—among other clients—you look after the financial affairs of a Mrs Patricia Roberts?'

'Yes, I've been acting for her for several years since her husband died.'

Jim now cleared his throat and forced himself to look Peter in the eye.

'Do you recall how much the firm invested for her—under your management?'

Peter researched his memory.

'Yes, I believe it's about a hundred thousand— quite a considerable investment'.

'The auditors have informed me that this money has been transferred into your bank account.

'This is alarming enough in itself—but, apparently, the funds have been transferred out of there to an offshore account in the Seychelles.'

Chapter Three

The trouble with expressions of surprise and alarm is that they could equally apply to guilt or innocence—alarm at being found out or having been wrongly accused.

As a prudent and responsible senior partner of a long-established law firm, it was understandable that Jim Preston should jump to the obvious conclusion.

'I am at a total loss to understand what motivated you in doing such a thing—unless you have been secretly harbouring a plan to do a bunk with these ill-gotten gains.'

Peter had not yet come to terms with the enormity of the accusation against him.

His only response—which appeared somewhat inadequate in the circumstances—was abject denial.

'I can assure you, Jim, that I know nothing whatsoever about this. I am as shocked as you are—when was the money transferred?'

'About a fortnight ago. It's just fortunate for the firm that the auditors happened to be here at this time—otherwise, it might not have been discovered.'

There was then a long and awkward pause.

Jim Preston could not look Peter in the eye.

'You realise what this means,' he said eventually.

'I have no choice as the firm's reputation is on the line. I have to suspend you from the partnership on a temporary basis until this is all cleared up one way or the other.'

Realising he was on thin ice, he then hastily added,

'I am not making any assumptions at this stage but I have to take precautions.'

It was clear to Peter that the meeting was at an end.

He rose slowly, shaking his head, turned and left the room.

On returning to his office, he found it difficult to decide what to do.

He heard his secretary, Patricia, busying herself next door in preparation for the day ahead.

He called her in and decided to bite the bullet.

She seemed perfectly normal and unprepared for the bombshell to come.

He invited her to sit down—unusual in itself.

'I have something to tell you,' he said. 'I want you to keep it to yourself but I'm sure word will spread like wildfire soon enough.

'Do you remember Mrs Patricia Roberts—one of my clients—I look after her investments?'

Patricia nodded.

'I've just learned that somebody transferred a hundred thousand of her assets into my bank account.'

Patricia looked apparently shocked.

'It gets worse—apparently, the money has been transferred to an account in the Seychelles.'

'How did this happen?' asked Patricia.

'I've no idea—but I want to assure you that it had nothing to do with me. Somebody got hold of my bank account. I don't understand how—surely nobody in the firm would do such a thing?'

Patricia nodded vigorously.

'Of course not. What is to happen now?'

'Unhappily—everyone will jump to the obvious conclusion. I have to leave the office until all this is sorted out one or another.

'You will have to make the excuse to my clients that I urgently needed a break for health reasons—but, of course, they'll find out the real reason soon enough'.

Peter realised that Patricia had suddenly dissolved into floods of tears.

'It will all come out in the wash—don't worry.'

He was far from sanguine that it would turn out that way.

Chapter Four

There was nothing for it but to pack up all his necessary bits and pieces and return home.

Rose was not due to arrive at school for her duties as secretary until later in the morning.

He drove the three miles home in a complete daze.

Everything was spinning around in his head.

It was a total nightmare.

As he pulled up on the drive, Rose glanced out of the window and concluded that he had forgotten to take some papers into the office.

She watched him get out of the car, and lean against it looking pale and confused.

He stumbled into the house and found her staring at him in the hallway.

'Is something wrong?' she asked.

He groped his way into the kitchen and reached up into a cupboard where he had secreted a bottle of malt.

He took a good swig, watched by an intrigued Rose.

'A bit early for that, isn't it, darling?'

He collapsed onto a kitchen chair and put his head in his hands.

'There's something seriously wrong,' said Rose, settling opposite him.

'You better get it off your chest.'

Peter tried to compose himself, but the effort was too much.

'It's just unbelievable,' he said. 'Someone has stolen a hundred thousand of a client's assets, put the money in our bank and then transferred the funds out of the country.

'The auditors spotted it this morning and Jim called me in to face me with it.

'He believes I stole the money.

'He's had to suspend me from the office pending further investigation.

'I've no idea how this could have happened—but someone has been very clever in accessing our account.

'Jim actually suggested that I had secreted it away prior to doing a bunk—of all things!

'How long have I been a partner?'

'Twenty years or so,' said Rose.

It was clear that she was finding it difficult to take the whole thing seriously.

'It will surely blow over—I mean, they can't really believe you would do such a thing—can they?'

'At the moment, I'm in the firing line unless they can come up with some other explanation. After all, I'm responsible for what goes into our bank—and what comes out.'

They sat there deep in thought.

'Who was the client?' asked Rose.

'A Mrs Patricia Roberts. I've been looking after her investments for three years since her husband died.

'She received a large inheritance so she won't miss the money—even such a large sum—but that is not the point.

'I'm responsible and the buck stops with me.'

'Will you have to tell her?' asked Rose.

'No, that will be up to Jim now—goodness knows what she'll think of me.'

The implications of what had happened were spreading as they spoke.

'So, you realise something else?' said Peter. 'The firm can't keep this under wraps. If it isn't sorted out in a day or so, they'll have to inform the police.

'I can't let this drag on without doing something to protect myself.

'If I don't hear by tomorrow evening that I'm off the hook, then I'll need someone I can trust to investigate. I know just the person.'

Chapter Five

The next day, there was an ominous silence and Peter could do nothing about it but wait for the inevitable.

Enough is enough, he thought, as he drove the following morning over to Robert's hotel.

He explained the whole problem to Robert over a strong coffee courtesy of Jean-Claude.

'The first thing the police will do is access your bank statements,' said Robert.

'Have you any idea at all who could be behind this?'

'Surely no one at the office,' said Peter.

'My secretary, Patricia, is quiet, single, lives on her own—wouldn't say boo to a goose—but a great secretary.

'When she heard what had happened, she burst into tears. She's been with me a long time.

'The cashier, Stuart, would have access to all my information but he's been with us an age and as straight as a die.'

'He'll be a key witness if this all goes ahead,' said Robert.

'Do you and Rose have separate accounts?'

'Yes, I don't know why we don't have a joint account—it's a bit old-fashioned of me, I suppose.

'Also, I still bank the old way—not online. Get regular written statements—I like to check them myself—though there's rarely anything to challenge— just old habits.'

'Nothing wrong with that,' said Robert.

'Would you hold my hand through all this—I really respect your expertise?'

'Of course. I'll start to make some discreet enquiries straight away.

'I think they'll let me sit in on your interview if I don't intervene. It would help me to see the way things are going and how you respond to questioning.'

'There's not much I can say besides professing my innocence.'

'All you can do now is go home and wait for the constabulary to call. It won't be long.'

They shook hands and Peter left.

Robert watched him drive away with sinking feelings.

He realised that this thing was going to get a lot worse before it got better.

When Peter arrived home, Rose told him that the police had already been in touch.

They wanted to interview him and suggested that he call at the station as soon as possible.

He called Robert and they arranged to meet in about thirty minutes—in the meantime, he confirmed this arrangement with the officer on the desk.

On arrival, he was met at the entrance by Detective Inspector Considine, accompanied by Detective Sergeant Draper.

Over the years, Peter had met the Inspector a couple of times—but on a social basis.

The officers both had a grave look, which did not bode well.

'I think you know what this is about,' said the Inspector. 'We would like to ask you some questions.'

'I hope you would not object to a friend, Robert Granger, being present on my behalf.'

The Inspector expressed some surprise.

'I have no objection, provided he merely observes.'

At this point, Robert arrived and joined them.

It was immediately apparent that both officers recognised him.

There was no obvious goodwill flowing.

They progressed through the inner workings of the station to a rather dingy interview room.

When they were seated, the Inspector indicated that he intended to conduct the interview under caution and on tape.

All four introduced themselves for the tape, before the Inspector began.

'I have asked you here because a large sum of money has gone missing from the account of a Mrs

Patricia Roberts—a client of your firm, Preston Downs, for which you has responsibility.

'This sum—a hundred thousand pounds—was transferred into your bank account and, subsequently, transferred to an account in the Seychelles, in other words, an offshore account.

'What is your explanation for this?'

Peter shook his head.

'I can't account for it. It has nothing to do with me. I did not withdraw the money. I know nothing about it.'

The Inspector gave Peter a quizzical look.

'You don't deny the facts are as I have stated.'

'Apparently not.'

'You know of no one who might have had your authority to withdraw these funds or to pay them into your account?'

The Inspector referred to papers in front of him.

'I have here your bank statements for the past year. There are a number of questions I need to ask you.'

Chapter Six

The Inspector produced the bank statements and passed them across to Peter.

'I'd like you to account for two large withdrawals over the past year. The first is thirty thousand pounds—rather a large sum.'

'My son, Clifford, ran into difficulties with his business—I paid him that sum to prevent his going bankrupt.'

'Very well, so you can explain why the sum of fifty thousand pounds was withdrawn a couple of months later?'

'That was a bank of mum and dad thing. My daughter, Clare, and her husband were short on their deposit for a new house.'

'Fair enough. However, you will see that this left you with less than ten thousand in the bank.'

The Inspector was leading up to making a point—Robert could see it coming a mile off.

'How old are you, Mr Compton?'

'Fifty-one.'

'Can I ask what provision—if any—you have made for your retirement?'

'None at the moment. I am receiving a decent share from the partnership—that's all.'

The Inspector leant back in his chair and looked satisfied.

'I suggest that these payments have reduced your savings drastically and that you saw a means of restoring your financial position by taking the money from your client's account.'

Peter bridled.

'Certainly not. I would never conceive of such a thing.'

'But you have no explanation as to how the money ended up in your account and then offshore?'

'I'm afraid I don't. It's a total mystery to me.'

The Inspector fixed Peter a piercing look.

'Peter Compton, I am placing you under arrest for the charge of theft.

'If you would come with me to see the custody sergeant I will arrange a formal charge and arrange bail pending further enquiries.'

In another twenty minutes, Peter and Robert left the station.

'Let's get a coffee in town,' Robert suggested.

'We need to see where we go from here.

'Obviously, I knew nothing about those withdrawals but you can see how the Inspector's mind is working.

'He now has the two things he needed—motive and opportunity.'

They drove into town and settled in a local café.

It was very quiet and Peter was relieved that he did not recognise anyone.

He had the uneasy feeling that everyone knew about him although this could not possibly be the case—yet.

'The fat is in the fire with a vengeance,' said Robert.

'The next stage will be an appearance before the local bench—they'll pass you up to the crown court.

'There's no way that magistrates will have jurisdiction.

'You're going to need a good criminal lawyer—I think we both know who I mean.'

Chapter Seven

It was clearly time for a strategy meeting.

Peter arrived at Robert's hotel the following morning bright and early.

They enjoyed one of Jean-Claude's excellent cooked breakfasts which set them up—in theory at least—for the day.

'We've ruled out the obvious suspects,' said Robert.

'However, it occurred to me that there may well have been others with evil intent who visited your office.

'Your partner who deals with criminal law—Jack Hills—may be prepared to give us names of criminal clients he has recently defended and who he met in the office.

'The layout of the office—isn't the toilet close to the cashier's room?

'If Stuart were out of the office for a time, one of them could have had access to his computer.

'It wouldn't take long for someone with expertise to get the info required.'

'It's certainly worth a shot,' said Peter.

'I'm sure Jack would give us the information on the QT.'

Robert paused to down a portion of bacon and egg.

'Next priority is to instruct Don Fingle on your behalf. He knows his way around all our courts.'

'He'll also know which counsel to instruct if things go that far.'

'I'll be before the bench and then transferred to crown court for pleas and directions. When I plead Not Guilty that will mean a trial and will delay the end date somewhat.'

'But time is obviously of the essence,' said Robert.

Peter returned home to find that Rose had left for work.

This, at least, was helping to keep her mind off things.

He searched in his diary to find the number for Stuart's private line.

Luckily, Stuart was not in court.

He had been sympathetic all along to Peter's problem and was only too ready to help.

'I can only think of three villains devious enough—and clever enough—to pull it off,' he said.

'I trust Robert Granger will be very discreet in his investigating; it must not get back to me in any circumstances—it would be a striking-off offence.'

'Understood,' said Peter. 'It's a long shot but I'm clutching at straws.'

'Well, good luck. When are you in court?'

'Any day now—I expect Considine to go ahead—you know him well enough. It's not often he gets someone like me in his sights.'

Peter returned to Robert and, over coffee, he gave him three names:

Jason Liddle

Kirk Runacres

Philip Stevens

All were men living locally and all had previous convictions, according to Stuart.

Robert made notes, and would shortly set about tracing these men and tracking them.

He knew from experience that, if one of them had pulled off such a stroke, there was no way they would not want to boast about it sooner or later to their muckers.

He had invested in a highly sophisticated device which enabled him to listen in to conversations over quite a distance—and to record them when necessary.

They decided to waste no time in contacting Don Fingle.

He was, as usual, in court, but his secretary—who had already heard about Peter's troubles on the legal grapevine—was only too willing to slot him into an afternoon appointment.

She knew it would be a feather in Don's cap to be representing such a high-profile local 'criminal'.

Chapter Eight

By mid-afternoon Peter and Robert were sitting rather tense waiting to see Don Fingle.

He suddenly burst into the waiting room.

Don was quite a character—somewhat rotund, with a moustache and ruddy face, usually full of smiles.

In his mouth was a large cigar.

'Well, well, well,' he exclaimed. 'I never thought I'd see you here—of all people—and I see you have Robert on board— a wise choice if I may say so.

'Come through—tea, do you?'

They both nodded and Don called his secretary to bring them all a cup.

Don seated himself behind a voluminous desk, the others seated facing him.

'You've been charged?' he asked.

'Yes, before the mags probably tomorrow, then on for plea and directions—next week?'

'Very probably. From what they tell me, this was a somewhat outlandish theft—don't tell me you actually did it?'

'Of course not,' said Peter, forcing a laugh.

'Robert here is trying to track down who is responsible.'

Don looked sceptical.

'We haven't got much time for that—even on a trial basis, you've likely to be reached in a couple of months. A few trials have gone short lately-'.

'Obviously, all the evidence points to me at the moment—and Considine thinks he has a clincher.

'He's spotted that I laid out most of my savings for family recently, leaving me very short, so he has a clear motive—he thinks.'

Don turned to Robert.

'So, it looks like it will be down to you to save the day,' he said.

The tea arrived and they paused for a drink.

'We had better get counsel on board as soon as possible.

'I can't think of anyone better than Hamish Mackie—a canny Scot who's been practising here and doing very well.

'I don't want to depress you but he's brilliant at mitigating—should it all go belly up.'

Don forced a kind of lethal smile.

'Let's be honest—if it all goes wrong what can I realistically expect?'

Don took a sip of his tea.

'Well, you're obviously going to be struck off the roll, lose your partnership—your whole career—and, of course, your good reputation. That's punishment enough but, for this—stealing money from a client—three to five years depending on the judge.'.

Peter's heart sank—but he had honestly been expecting it.

'You don't think they'll bring in anyone heavyweight?'

'I shouldn't think so—but I'd rather have a regular than some recorder out of his depth and out to make a name for himself,' said Don.

'I'll see you tomorrow morning to take instructions. I need to know how your office accounts work—more about the client who lost her money. Anything you think might help.'

Peter and Robert left the office.

Don contacted Hamish Mackie's clerk and booked a conference in chambers for the following week; by then he would have detailed instructions from Peter.

Chapter Nine

Robert now set to work urgently to track down Jason Liddle, Kirk Runacres and Philip Rankin.

He discovered that Jason Liddle lived alone and frequented a local pub where he seemed to be popular with the regulars.

Following at a careful distance, he entered the pub, bought a drink and moved to another part of the bar where he had a clear view of Jason but would not attract attention.

His recording device was secreted but aimed across the bar in Jason's direction.

There was the usual joshing between mates and plenty of man-style boasting about their various relationships with local women.

Nothing about his demeanour or casual attitude gave any indication that he might have been involved in something so technical as the office theft—and, frankly, he did not seem to have the bottle for such a venture.

Robert was quick to rule him out of the game.

He left the pub after only one pint and turned his attention to Kirk Runacres.

He called it a day and returned to the hotel and its more salubrious surroundings.

The following morning, Peter attended before the magistrates where he was swiftly moved on to the crown court, his bail being extended but, at the prosecution's request, two conditions were added—without protest from Peter.

The first was that he should not have contact with any partner or member of staff at Preston Downs—to prevent possible interference with prosecution witnesses.

The second—perhaps rather unnecessary—was to report each day to the police station at six p.m.

DI Considine was clearly determined to view him as a possible fugitive.

The magistrates refrained from looking at him directly. The local press were there in force to gloat.

Peter felt acutely the absence of Robert and his reassuring presence, although Don put in a brief appearance to see that the formalities were observed.

The conference in chambers with Hamish Mackie was the following day, and Robert would be there this time to lend support.

Meanwhile, Robert spent some time racking down Kirk Runacres.

He was a very different animal from Jason.

He lived in quite a respectable flat with a long-term girlfriend Linda.

She was a 'meeter and greeter' in a local club of a somewhat dubious reputation.

They owned a fairly ancient car which was parked in the street outside the flat—too old to be of any interest to the local youths intent on pilfering and criminal damage.

Robert kept watch in the evening and saw them leave in the car and drive to a café, where they met up with two other couples.

Again, he was able to settle at a table with an uninterrupted view and to record their conversation.

There was nothing said that raised his suspicions, although they briefly discussed Peter's case and took the opportunity of pouring opprobrium on him.

Robert had to conclude that this couple were highly unlikely to be involved anyway in the enterprise.

He realised that he was running out of options and hoped for better luck with Philip Rankin.

Chapter Ten

Peter and Robert arrived in chambers for the pre-trial conference with Hamish Mackie.

They were led into a very smart room; most of the walls decorated with law books and the regulation statutes in leather-bound editions.

Hamish came forward to greet them with a wide smile.

He was not tall but gave the impression of being extremely robust, and full of suppressed energy.

He shook hands with Peter and stared openly at him for a few moments.

'I like to do this with all my clients,' he said. 'I can pick up so much from those first few moments—even guilt or innocence seems to emanate.'

'I hope you concluded the latter,' Peter replied.

'Of course, I'm not here to decide that—it's for a jury. On this occasion, however, I can confirm that my first impressions have been universally favourable.

'The trouble is that my opposite number may have something of an open goal in front of him here—unless you can point the finger at someone else.

'There's a Latin maxim—'res ipsa loquitur'—which you both know well.

'If it wasn't you who did the deadly deed—then who was it?'

'That is what I'm determined to find out,' said Robert. 'Robert Granger, by the way, private investigator—officially retired—but an old friend of Peter's.'

They shook hands.

'Time is short. There'll be a plea and directions tomorrow—your Not Guilty plea will ensure that we have at least a short interval before the trial.

'I've read the brief—we have to make bricks with very little straw here—but your good reputation and character will help—also the points that the prosecution intend to make about your generosity to your son and daughter may well redound in your favour.

'If the worst comes to the worst, there are bags of mitigation—you have already been punished and a great deal more is to come.

'A sensible judge will pick up on that and realise that a prison sentence is nothing more than to satisfy public expectation and to discourage others.'

'Nevertheless, not very reassuring,' said Peter.

'I have to be honest, we don't have a good defence—but I'll do everything I possibly can.'

Robert and Peter left with a good deal to think about.

The following day—as predicted—Peter entered his plea and the case was adjourned.

Meanwhile, Robert had tracked down the last of his possible suspects—Philip Rankin.

Of the three, he was clearly the most sophisticated and had been convicted of computer fraud.

Not for him a local pub but the best hotel in town.

Robert saw him join two other men at the bar and order whisky and sodas.

He tuned in, as usual, from a chair near the entrance.

There were other murmurs of conversation but he was able to isolate what Philip and his friends were saying.

There was a lot of technical chatter about computers, then he distinctly heard Philip,

'Did you read about that lawyer? They say he was caught by an audit, otherwise, they might never have known about it.'

'You can't trust lawyers with your money,' another commented.

They went on with other conversation and Robert decided that he had better call it a day.

It was clear that none of the three men he had been tracking were involved.

Chapter Eleven

The date for Peter's trial was fixed—listed for two days in a fortnight.

Robert had reported back over another hearty breakfast at the hotel, but Peter had begun to lose his appetite.

He had no idea how he was going to get through that period—anxiously waiting for what seemed like the inevitable, made far worse by knowing that he was innocent.

Whenever he ventured into town he felt obliged to avoid any of his old haunts

He found that friends he met in the street were turning away to avoid contact.

He had the ghastly feeling that all fingers were pointing at him and accusing him.

He longed to see Mrs Roberts and try to explain to her that he had always looked after her investments with total honesty—but he was prevented even from that by the fact that she was a prosecution witness.

The days ticked by. Rose did her best to cheer him up but it was no good.

He started to sort out details of the domestic expenses that he dealt with but knew that Rose would manage perfectly well without him.

Would anyone apart from Rose and the family really care—his secretary, Patricia, had been in tears when he left the office, and he and Robert had seen her coming along the street one day.

He longed to reassure her and could see that she was very distressed.

Robert felt that his failure to come up with any suspect reflected on his professional ability.

It was not often he faced abject failure, and the more so when the chips were really down.

On the weekend before the trial, it rained heavily.

Robert decided that he needed a good stiff drink.

In the early evening, he resorted to a downtown pub where he knew that the atmosphere would at least be uplifting.

He settled near the car and noticed a couple nearby.

The man, bearded but possessing a certain swagger even seated, struck a chord in Robert's memory.

Where had he seen him before—and not in a pleasant setting?

Now, it dawned on him—Darren Black—the beard had thrown him off for a moment.

A womaniser with a reputation. Opposite sat a woman clearly in distress.

He could not see her face, but he could not avoid hearing her desperate pleas.

'Darren, I had to see you—I missed you-'

'I told you to stay away until I got in touch.'

'But I love you, Darren—I want to be with you-'

His expression told the story.

He had lost interest in her and she was now an embarrassment.

Robert craned round to see the woman's face.

The shock was complete.

It was Pat—Peter's secretary. He had no doubt of it.

What on earth was she doing with a lowlife like Darren?

He still had his listening device and quickly switched it on.

'I only did it for you-' she pleaded.

'I told you to lie low until I got in touch. When your boss goes down and the coast is clear—we'll get away. The money is all secure. It will be the good life from then on.'

'Do you still love me?' There was total desperation in her voice.

'Of course,' he lied. 'Now don't bother me again until I ring you.'

Robert turned away quickly. They had not noticed him.

Now it was all clear to him.

Poor Patricia had somehow become involved with Darren—a single girl, vulnerable, probably never had a steady boyfriend—and putty in his hands

Of course, she had ready access to all the data he required and no one suspected her.

Robert knew he had the clincher, rang Peter, who was totally surprised, and they arranged a meeting at the Police Station with DI Considine.

He listened to the recording in complete silence.

'You're a lucky son of a gun,' he commented.

Chapter Twelve

They picked up Patricia and she told them the whole story, sobbing with guilt as she went.

They picked up Darren Black, who never realised what had hit him.

The charge against Peter was withdrawn, but he knew that he would always be referred to as that lawyer accused of stealing from his client.

Jim Preston was mightily relieved—not so much for Peter but for his firm's reputation.

Robert was able to settle down to a quiet life again—vindicated—but knew that luck had played the vital part.

Peter lost no time in arranging to visit Mrs Roberts.

She was sweetness itself.

'I never missed the money—but I always felt so dreadful for you—what you must have been through.'

There was sympathy there – but had she really believed his innocence?

That was another story.

Paradise is a Myth

Chapter One

It was a bright, late June morning with the sun already making its presence felt at 7.30 am. Robert Grainger was up early as usual, and had decided to have a swim in the sea before indulging in one of Jean-Claude's superb cooked breakfasts.

No one else was around as he entered the dining room and exited through the double doors on to the patio. He was in light daps and threaded his way through the garden and out towards the beach.

The was one other elderly resident, Peter House, a retired physician who usually rose about 8.30 am and sometimes coincided with Robert for a few choice words. It was usually unlikely that any holidaymakers passing through would be around before the school holidays and the two of them had the place to themselves.

Robert arrived at the beach and shed his few clothes. His usual practice was to take off at a run and plough into the waves. That way the shock of the temperature was very much reduced. Having swum with a vigorous crawl. He found himself some thirty metres out and turned on his back to enjoy the sunshine. It was then he noticed for the first time, an object bobbing about some ten metres away. He turned and went to investigate.

To his surprise, it was a glass bottle inside of which something was scrawled on a piece of paper. He strained to make out what was written, in longhand, but could not make it out clearly. Heading for the shore, he discovered that the bottle had a metal stopper which came away easily enough. Sitting alone on the beach, he felt inside and removed the message.

In black ink it read: *If you find this, please help me. I am in great danger but the police won't help and I have no one to turn to. Please ring my mobile* (and the number was clearly written).

The message was not signed and it was impossible to know whether it emanated from a man or a woman. Robert's long experience as a private detective told him with fair certainty that the sender was likely to be a woman. What man would have written such a message, leaving it being found purely to fate? He rose and went back to his suite on the first floor of the hotel.

These days, his life had descended into a fair degree of monotony and the thought of following up on this message was quite alluring. After all, he had nothing to lose if it turned out to be a practical joke. He was not going anywhere and perhaps the message was really genuine, a woman in distress which was right up his street.

He dialled the number and waited for several seconds before his call was picked up. A female voice, sounding quite young, answered. 'So, you found my message?'

'Yes, when did you leave it?'

'Yesterday morning. I had no idea whether it would be found. It really was a last resort.'

'Are you as desperate as you say? Who are you?'

There was a pause. Robert imagined she was assessing from his voice and his answers whether or not she could trust him Evidently she decided it was worth taking a chance.

'I'm Linda. Who are you?'

There seemed to be nothing to gain by Robert prevaricating. 'I'm Robert Grainger. You may have struck lucky as I am a retired private investigator. I don't know your situation but I will help in any way I can.'

There was another pause while Linda considered his response. Finally, she sighed audibly. 'I doubt you will be able to help but it's worth a shot. Are you on the island?'

'Yes, where are you?'

'I'm on the move. I suggest we meet at the ferry terminal at Yarmouth, say 12 O'clock. Can you do that?'

'Yes, but how will we recognise one another?'

Linda paused then replied, 'I don't think that will be a problem,' and rang off.

Chapter Two

Robert had long since ceased to drive. Instead he relied on his very good friend and local taxi driver, Bill, to ferry him around the island when the need arose. They had history together having recently toured the mainland in an effort to rescue his errant son. Bill arrived in time for one of Jean-Claude's barista style coffees and one of his superb croissants with butter and local honey.

'You do yourself pretty well here, Robert,' he remarked, nodding to Jean-Claude as he made a graceful departure.

'Wouldn't change a thing,; said Robert, finishing his mouthful.

'Where are we off to this time?' Bill enquired, expecting no conventional response, on past experience.

'Something very curious; Robert began, explaining his swim and the discovery in a bottle. "She sounded genuinely frightened. We might be able to sort it out. I agreed to meet at twelve at the Yarmouth ferry terminal.'

'Description?' asked Bill.

'No idea but she sounded quire young.'

They cleared the decks and set off giving themselves plenty of time to recce the area.

The sun was shing brightly and the traffic quite light. Bill pulled up a little way from the terminal and they set off to see who might be waiting for them. A ferry had just departed for the mainland and there was no one around.

They settled nearby to watch for anyone female approaching but 12 o'clock came and went with no sign of the elusive Linda.

There was however, a rather down and out young fellow with a heavy beard, who kept gazing at them. He then approached in a gingerly fashion. 'Robert Grainger?' he enquired. 'I've got a message for you from Linda.'

Robert nodded.

'Change of plan,' he said. 'Meet at Warren Farm café by the Needles. One o'clock. Don't ask me, she gave me a tenner to pass on the message.' With that he slunk off without turning round.

'She's being ultra cautious,' Robert remarked. 'It sounds as though she has someone very close on her trail. Warren Farm if fairly isolated. No one going in or out is likely to avoid being spotted.'

They set off and a few minutes later drew up at the farm café. There were two cars parked. It was just past 1 pm so they assumed one of the cars belonged to Linda

They approached the entrance as a young, blonde woman in a T-shirt and jeans appeared, hesitated for a moment and then came up.

'Somehow didn't expect you to arrive in a taxi. Which of you is Robert?'

He held out a hand which she shook vigorously. She looked around anxiously. 'Sure you weren't followed?'

Robert shook his head. 'We would have spotted anyone on our tail. Let's go inside and you can start to explain what this is all about.'

Chapter Three

They settled at a table and Robert was able to appraise Linda for the first time. She was, he guessed, in her early twenties and was attractive with a face that appeared lived in for her age.

She in her turn was able to see Robert and Bill for the first time, as a couple of older men but still vigorous and fit.

Robert ordered coffees all round and noted that Bill and Linda were obviously chatting in quite a relaxed way. He brought a tray to the table and there was a silence as they prepared to drink.

'You must think I'm round the bend for putting that message in a bottle,' she said. 'I wouldn't have done it if I hadn't been quite desperate. Quite honestly I never expected anyone to respond.'

'Just a bit of luck thaat I happened to be having my early morning swim,' Robert replied.

'So, you were a private detective.'

'Still am when the need arises.'

Linda seemed impressed

'And do you work together?'

Robert looked at Bill before replying. 'Not exactly. I gave up driving after I came to the island. Bill runs a taxi and ferries me around. He's a very good friend.'

Linda seemed reassured by this and noticeably relaxed. 'I thinks it's time I explained myself,' she said 'It's difficult to know where to start. About two years ago I was living on my own and scraping a living at menial jobs, earning scarcely enough to pay the rent on my grotty flat.

'My grandfather, Jim, was living on his own in quite a large house. He had been widowed for some years. I visited him about twice a month and realised he was becoming quite frail. He had been extremely independent in looking after himself. I felt sorry for him and began to visit more often until I became almost like a housekeeper.

'My parents divorced when I was young, I was brought up by my mother and my three brothers by my father's second wife who wanted nothing to do with me as I grew up.

They also had little if anything to do with their grandfather. About six months ago, Jim became very ill and I looked after him every day. He told me that he hadn't made a will but that he had some savings which he kept hidden in the house. The house was rented so these savings were the only asset that he was able to pass to the family.

'The three boys must have got wind that he was on his way out and they started turning up and making a fuss of him. I realised they were hoping to cash in when he passed away.'

Robert and Bill had been giving her their rapt attention. 'Had they found out about the savings?' asked Robert

'They were snooping about and I think they discovered his building society book. He was quite old fashioned and kept his money in a current account.'

'Did you discover how much he had saved p?'

He told me it was forty thousand, and he was leaving it all to me.'

'That must have been a surprise,' said Robert.

'I arranged his funeral, nobody came but the three boys.'

'And the cash?'

'I had removed the box and had it in my flat. I don't have a bank account. The boys were canny and I found out they were following me. They must have suspected I had the money.

'I was in the local pub when one of them cornered me and said they knew I had the money and were entitled to a quarter share each. I denied it but he said they would follow me until I owned up and gave them their fair share.

'He was very frightening. I had no one to help me and I was afraid to go to the police, after all, what could they do?

'In despair one day, I was on the beach at Sandown and wrote the message and threw the bottle into the sea.'

'Were you still in possession of the cash?' asked Robert

'Yes but this is where I'll need your help.

Chapter Four

For one moment, Robert thought she was going to say she had the money with her.

Then he realised that with the boys tracking her it was highly unlikely that she would take such a chance.

'It may seem crazy but I realised that if I could just elude them somehow long enough to hide the money, I could go back later and retrieve it,' said Linda. 'I split the money up into four bags, you'd be surprised how little room fifty pound notes take up.'

Now came the sixty-four thousand dollar question. 'So, they're hidden somewhere on the island?' asked Robert.

'No, I took a day trip to the mainland, one of them was watching me but dared not approach as I kept with a crowd of passengers. In Lymington I ran and managed to jump on a bus before he could follow.'

This story was getting more bizarre by the minute. 'So, where did you end up?' asked Robert.

'Somewhere near Sway. I got off when I saw woodland and it gave me the idea.'

'Don't tell me you hid it in the woods?'

'I walked for a bit and checked there was no one around. Then I dug holes in the ground with my bare hands and buried each of the four bags. I marked the spot by a particular tree. It was unusual and I'm sure I would recognise it again.'

'The we had better go and find the money as soon as possible and put it in a bank.'

'You know I don't have an account.'

'You'll just have to trust me. I can deposit it for you, that's the only way the money is going to be safe. If one of the boys catches up with you he may force you to reveal where you hid it.'

Linda was looking rather doubtful. 'I've only just met you and you're asking me to trust you with all the money?'

'Don't worry, I will give you a proper receipt.'

They finished their drinks.

'We had better get over to the mainland as soon as possible. Let's hope your memory is good. You need to tell us where you got off the bus near Sway.'

They managed to catch a boat to Lymington and set off on the minor road towards Sway.

'There's a bus coming the other way,' Robert remarked, 'which proves we're on a bus route, hopefully the one you were on, Linda.

'Now keep your eyes peeled. Did you request the driver to stop at a specified bus stop?'

'Yes,' said Linda. 'When I saw the woods either side of the road I decided that would do,'

They were travelling quite slowly and rather holding up the traffic.

'Do you recognise any landmarks so far?' asked Bill. 'We're entirely in your hands here.'

Suddenly Linda pointed at a bus stop some fifty metres ahead. 'I'm, pretty sure this is where I got off.'

Bill saw theere was a narrow turning into the woods on the left, gave a belated signal causing the driver behind to blare his horn, and swung off the road. They parked and got out.

'There's a path down there. I recognise that is where I started walking. There was no one about.'

They diligently followed the path as it wound into the woods which were becoming deeper.

'I'm looking for a certain tree.' Linda was leading them along looking from left to right, when she suddenly stopped. 'I'm sure that's it.' She pointed to a gnarled old elm about five metres in from the track.

Robert watched in fascination as Linda dug rapidly with her fingers in the soft earth. After a few moments, she gave a cry of triumph and held up a small cotton bag. She handed it to Robert and he immediately saw that it was stuffed with fifty pound notes. She knelt back down and started feeling in the earth.

After a few moments, three other similar bags appeared, all similarly containing notes. Robert recalled that she had commented how little room ten thousand pound of fifty pound notes took up. Two hundred new notes bound together. Yet somehow the notes stuffed into these bags seemed bulkier. Was Linda telling them the whole truth?

Chapter Five

Confident that they had not been followed, they returned to Bill's taxi and made their way back to the ferry port.

Robert had brought a stout leather bag with him to secrete the spoils.

Throughout the crossing, Linda became increasingly nervous, searching the faces of the passengers in case any of the three brothers were on board.

Nothing was heard or seen to rouse their suspicions as they followed a line of traffic off into the shore and set out for Robert's hotel.

'I have a spare room in my suite,' Robert declared, 'I don't suppose you have anywhere to stay.'

Linda appeared relieved and grateful for the offer. 'Are you sure I won't be too much trouble?' she asked

'Depends on what plans you have. We had better go to my bank tomorrow and pay in the money before the brothers track you down again.'

'Aren't they going to wonder where all that cash came from?' Bill enquired.

'Money laundering regs are pretty strict but I know my bank staff and I don't anticipate any trouble there,' said Robert with a smile. 'Linda, you must come with me of course, to see everything is above board. The money will be on deposit, it won't earn anything much these days. The main thing is to put it beyonds harm's way.'

They arrived at the hotel as darkness fell on a beautiful evening.

'Thanks for everything, Bill. Let me settle up now.'

Robert waved away his protestations, paid the fair and added a good tip.

They entered the hotel as Bill drove away, to be greeted by Jean-Claude

'This is Linda. She'll be staying with me as my guest for the time being.'

The soul of discretion, Jean-Clade merely gave a slight nod as they passed him on the way to the stairs.

'I'm absolutely exhausted,' said Linda as Robert showed her to his spare room.

'You can crash out in here. I'm always up early for a swim but I'll only wake you for one of Jean-Claude's special breakfasts in bed.'

With this thrilling prospect in view, Linda yawned deeply, wished him goodnight and closed the door.

Before retiring himself, Robert emptied the bag and decided to check the money for himself. As he had suspected, when it came to counting fifty pound notes, it was no surprise that the total far surpassed the figure

Linda had been suggesting. Laid out on his bed it came to eighty thousand pounds. Robert had long ceased to be surprised at being misled. It was after all the daily diet of a private detective. The revelation had however given him thought. It would be prudent for the time being to play along with Linda's version.

Presumably the three avaricious brother had also been led to believe the total was forty.

Chapter Six

Having replaced the bank notes and locked his bag carefully, Robert retired to bed having hidden the bag away as safely as he could.

He had no way of knowing whether any of the three brothers had followed them off the boat from Lymington. They may have seen the involvement of Bill and himself and decided to bide their time. Jean-Claude had shown on other occasions that he was quite able to defend the hotel and its residents against intruders.

The following morning he rose in the early hours and could detect no nise of any kinnd from the next door bedroom.

He slipped out of the hotel by the back entrance and headed for the beach, There was no one in sight as he ran into the waves and felt the exhilerating rush of the cold sea water on his skin.

He swam strongly for a few minutes, then relaxed and lay on his back contemplating how the day might work out. Strange to think it was only a day or so since he had chanced on the bottle with Linda's note inside.

It was a weekday so he would be able to accompany her to his bank and pay in the money. He was still convinced that it was strategically important not to let on that he had discovered her deception. His instinct told him that this was the case – something that he could not explain that emanated from life experiences.

Half an hour later he left the water, dried himself off and returned to his suite. There was still no sign of Linda.

He tiptoed downstairs and found Jean-Claude busy in the kitchen. 'My guest is still sleeping but when she wakes perhaps you could prepare one of your special fried breakfasts. I'll check with her first, of course. I remember that she drinks coffee so a nice cafetiere would be welcome.'

When he returned to his suite, he heard the unmistakable sounds of Linda moving about. He tapped on the door. 'Jean-Claude is cooking up a superb English fry and coffee, you are welcome to have it in your room.'

There was a pause before Linda poked her head round the door. 'Are you sure? That would be great but aren't you spoiling me? I could get used to all this.'

'All part of the service,' said Robert, smiling.

Within a few minutes all was prepared and Robert pottered downstairs to his own breakfast.

The other retired resident, physician, Peter House, was seated at one end of the table reading *The Times* and chewing on a buttered croissant. 'Morning, Robert,' he ventured, casting a beady eye on the younger man. 'Been out for your usual early swim?' There was a hint of envy there.

'Very refreshing,' Robert replied, 'you should try it.'

'I'll settle for looking at it, thank you,' he smiled, turning away ostentatiously to study the financial section of his paper. 'I hear you have a young female guest,' he remarked without looking up.

Robert was not going to rise to this. 'A friend of the family. Only here for a few days.' That seemed to shut him up.

Jean-Claude arrived with the sumptuous cooked breakfast and there was silence as he ate hungrily, planning his strategy for the day ahead.

Chapter Seven

At about ten, Robert phoned for Bill to collect them in half an hour for the trip to Robert's bank in Newport. It was already warm and getting warmer, with a hot sun and no breeze.

'Could you hang on for us for half an hour or so?' asked Robert as they alighted outside his bank.

Once inside, Robert suggested that Linda could take a seat while he sought an interview with his favourite bank clerk. He had done her some favours in the past in ridding her of a pestiferous ex-boyfriend and now was the time to return the favour, accept the deposit with no questions asked. She ushered him into her small office and he took a seat.

'I have rather a lot of cash in this bag,' he began. 'Can you put it in my deposit account? I assure you there is nothing dishonest going on but obviously money laundering questions would normally be asked. I shall be withdrawing it very shortly but it needs a safe home for the time being.'

Judith gave a sardonic smile, took the bag from him and looked inside.

'Eighty thousand in fifties, a bequest to my client from a dying uncle who kept it all under the bed.'

Judith gave him a sceptical look but emptied the bag, gave a low whistle, amd proceeded to parcel it up. Expertly dividing it into tens of thousands.

'I will need some sort of receipt to show my friend that it is all above board.'

Judith nodded and a receipt was made out.

'Could you produce a copy for me?' he asked.

It was all accomplished within minutes.

Robert returned to the foyer with the empty bag and sat next to Linda. 'Here's a receipt,' he said, passing it over without drawing attention to the total set out. To his surprise, Linda simply opened her bag and put the folded receipt inside. Could trust go any further than this, Robert mused to himelf.

'The money is safely on deposit so no one can get at it. We had not discussed what is to happen to you now?'

Linda pulled a face. 'I suppose I'd better return to my flat. I shall miss being with you and Bill. You've both been so kind to me. I'll keep in touch and let you know when I decide what to do with the money.'

'What about the brothers? They know where you live.'

Linda pulled a face. 'I don't think they would try to break in, my neighbours have been alerted and they are looking for strangers lurking about. I think I can take care of myself.'

Robert loooked rather sceptical. 'Well you know where to get hold of me – any time day or night – in a crisis.

Without warning, she came up and gave him a big hug.

Chapter Eight

Things settled down after that for a few days. Robert was able to get down to some serious reading, as he parked himself in a shady spot in the hotel's capacious garden. Every now and then he exchanged some desultory chat with the hotel's gardner, Joseph, as he pottered about watering and weeding.

There was a lull before the school holidays when all was calm and serene.

A week or so went by and apart from a shopping expedition with Bill into Newport, there was nothing dramatic to report. He had heard not a word from Linda. Presumably she was looking for a job and would not want to start spending any of her inheritance just yet, although the temptation to go on a bit of a spending spree must have been very great.

He was settling down after a Jean-Claude special breakfast one morning, when the man himself sidled up. 'Someone is trying to contact you, mon ami,' he whispered. 'A rather strange phone call asking if I could put the caller in touch with you as he had something rather important to tell you.'

Robert took the note containing the number. 'I don't recognise this,' he remarked. 'Perhaos I'll wait to see if the caller rings again. Logically he will if the information is important enough. I'm just wary of cold calls. It's usually trouble.'

Sure enough an hour later, Jean-Claude appeared again, the caller seemed more serious this time. 'OK, leave it with me,' said Robert.

He dialled the number which appeared to be a mobile. It rang for a few moments but was then answered by a rather muffled male voice. Robert recognised a rather feeble attempt at disguise. 'Got someone here who'd like to talk to you.'

There was a pause and what appeared to be some sort of scuffle going on. A rather desperate Linda came on the phone. 'They've locked me up. I can't see a thing and don't know where I am.' She was in tears and obviously very frightened.

Don't tell me, it's the brothers,' said Robert rather resignedly. He had been waiting for them to make a move.

'We just want what's rightly ours,' said the voice.

'And you think this is the right way to get it?' asked Robert. 'Kidnap is a very serious offence.'

There was the sound of laughter at the other end and a discussion going on.

'Sounds as though you are all in this together,' said Robert.

'We'll release her on condition that we each receive our fair share. Ten thousand apiece or you may never see her again.'

Robert could hear Linda's startled reaction to this. She came back on the phone, 'They're pretty desperate. They're threatening to harm me,'

Robert replied as calmly as he could, 'They won't harm you, there's too much at stake.'

'What are you going to do?'

'I'll think about it.'

He rang off.

Chapter Nine

Robert decided to make them sweat for a while. He enjoyed a full cafetiere of Jean-Claude's excellent coffee and sat outside in the sun to enjoy it. After a hour or so, he rang the number again.

He was met with the aggravated tones of one of the brothers, 'You took your time,' he said.

'I didn't think there was any time limit,' Robert replied.

'So here's the deal. We collect the thirty grand from you and we release Linda, in that order.'

Robert paused to consider. 'She must be released unharmed, and if you try to renege of the deal, the police will move in straight away. They know me here and they will proceed against all three of you, you can guarantee it.'

He heard them talking to Linda who was clearly unimpressed. She came on the phone. 'I'm not happy about this. I don't trust them

Robert paused before replyinng. 'Listen, we have to do it this way. You know that if we don't you are never going to have a quiet moment. Just trust me. I'm concerned about your safety.'

'Then I'll leave it to you but I hope I won't live to regret it.'

He then heard Linda shouting at one of them to take his hands off her. She was showing plenty of spirit.

'Where shall we do the handover of the money?' the brother asked impatiently.

'You know the location of my hotel,' said Robert. 'Meet me there in three hours. I'll have the money and Linda had better be unharmed.'

He rang off and called Bill. 'Need to call at my bank as soon as possible.'

Bill arrived after about ten minutes and as they journeyed to the bank, Robert made a call to the clerk who had handled the cash. He remembered she had bagged the money in bundles of ten thousand which would be very useful now. She was not surprised when he informed her that he wanted to withdraw all the money at once. It had become rather embarrassing in case anyone above her found out.

As anticipated, the money was bagged and ready for collection.

They drove back to the hotel and Robert suggested that Bill should stick around until the collection was made.

In fact, one of the brothers arrived within two hours. The three of them sat at a table and Robert produced three bags which he emptied. The brother, who seemed to be barely in his early twenties, launched himself at the cash greedily. 'It's all there,' said Robert, 'but you had better count it anyway.'

As the brother gathered up the bag to leave, Robert got up and looked him in they eye. Bill was seated watching, but very alert. 'That's our part of the deal. Where is Linda?'

'You'll find her waiting on the front at Ventnor, at three o'clock.

Robert pointed a finger at him. 'You had better be right. Therre'll be no second chances. Now get out.'

He turned his back and the brother slunk out.

'A most unpleasant piece of work,' Bill remarked.

'Now that's behind us let me invite you to join me in a spot of lunch.'

Chapter Ten

They set off together about half past two with some trepidation. As they turned down towards the front at Ventnor they could see a small figure sitting quietly alone. The parked and approached quietly.

Linda got up and threw her arms around Robert who was quite taken aback. 'I don't think you'll see much more of them,' said Robert. 'They've got what they were after all along.'

Linda was recovering fast. 'You seemed to give in to them very quickly,' she said.

Robert looked her in the eye. 'There are two things I can say to that. First, you need to look at the situation practically. They were never going to give up pestering and threatening you. You would've ended up always looking over your shoulder. Secondly, I'm afraid you've not been honest with me.'

Linda feigned shock. 'What do you mean?'

'A small matter of the amount of your inheritance. You told me it was forty thousand. I believed you until I checked for myself. In fact it's eighty thousand.'

Linda looked crestfallen.

'Now do you understand why I was ready to do a deal with the brothers? They are still under the impression that they have received a quarter. In fact you are walking away with fifty thousand. Considerably more that the total you told me about.

'I would call that a pretty good result, wouldn't you?'